Protecting the Prin____ ____ ___ ____ great read from Carol Moncado and a great addition to the Monarchies of Belles Montagnes Series. My favorite character created in this book by Ms. Moncado is Michaela. She is such a devoted, caring, giving, loving person! She was willing to give up everything for her charge...thinking nothing of what she had to give up of herself, but always thinking of others. This is a heartwarming story that gets you all excited for the next story in this series Prince from her Past. I can't wait to hear the story of Prince Nicklaus and Princess Yvette.

— RH

Protecting
the Prince

Carol
Moncado

USA Today Bestselling Author

CANDID
Publications

Cover photos: Copyright: ruslan117/ depositphotos.com
    Author photo: Captivating by Keli, 2010
    First edition, CANDID Publications, 2015

Tony Browning stepped off the plane in Athmetica, the capital city of the Sovereign Commonwealth of Athmetis. The unseasonable weather caused heat to roil off the tarmac in visible waves and threatened to give Tony heat stroke. The suit he wore was suitable for the current weather in Ravenzario but much too warm for Athmetis. Why hadn't he thought to check the temperature?

For this trip, he was on his own. No chauffeur would meet him at the airport. No car would whisk him away to his destination. In fact, no one official knew he was here. He'd used his position as Queen Christiana's head of security to gain diplomatic status in the island nation, but only because it afforded him less hassle. If, as he suspected, he ended up in the United States, he'd travel even more conventionally.

Once through the airport, skipping baggage claim, he hailed a taxi and took it to the hotel, in a village a few kilometers away, where he'd stay for the next couple of days.

If he couldn't find any sign of the young prince and his nanny here, he'd move on to the next location on his list.

"Sir?"

Tony blinked as the driver got his attention. "Yes?"

"We've arrived."

He shook himself out of his stupor. "My apologies." Tony started to open the door, but paused. "Are you familiar with this area?"

"Of course!" His chest puffed up, as though offended Tony would ask such a thing. "I rode my bike around the entire village as a child. You want to go somewhere, I know the best way to get there."

"You grew up here?" Could this be the stroke of luck he needed?

"Two streets over. My Yaya worked at this very hotel."

"What's your name?"

"Rex Cromer, sir."

"Rex, can I hire you for the next couple of days?" Confusion filled the other man's face. "I need a guide who knows this area well. You would need to be on call twenty-four hours a day, but you will be well-compensated." Tony named a figure he knew would entice the other man.

"What's the catch?" Rex's eyes narrowed.

"No catch. I'm doing research into some people I believe came here in late 1999 or very early 2000. I need to find them. They may or may not still be in the area, but if at all possible, I need to know where they went."

Could Rex's eyes narrow any further? "Why? Are you a hit man?"

Tony laughed. "Quite the opposite. They ran from a family member who was quite dangerous. He has finally been put in prison for life. It is safe for them to come home, but no one knows exactly where they are anymore. I know where their first destination, here in Athmetis was supposed to be, but beyond that, we don't know." Time to lay most of the cards on the table. "To be honest I'm not even completely sure what names they used, just that they didn't use their real names."

He could see Rex turn the proposal over in his head. "Very well. You were to have been my last fare for the day, and I have two days off. You should talk to my Yaya. She's known everyone in this area for the last sixty years or longer."

Within ten minutes, Tony had been ushered into Yaya's home. After exchanging pleasantries, he got down to business, pulling photos out of his pocket. "Do you remember seeing either of these people around the turn of the century?"`

Yaya took the photos and examined them carefully with the help of a magnifying glass. "So young," she murmured as she held the photo of Prince Nicklaus. "So sad."

"So sad?" Tony's heart constricted. Had something happened to the prince and his caretaker in the intervening years? They hadn't even considered that possibility.

"So sad his parents died so young." She looked up and stared Tony in the eyes. "His sister and he were the only remaining members of their immediate family, no?"

She knew? How?

Yaya must have seen the questions in his eyes. "Rex, please get our guest something to drink."

"Of course, Yaya." His gaze shifted between Tony and his grandmother, but he left.

"Who are you?" she demanded as soon as Rex was out of earshot. "Why do you want to know about these two people?"

Tony pulled out his credentials. "I am the head of Queen Christiana of Ravenzario's security detail, ma'am."

She took them and examined them closely. Satisfied, she returned them. "Very well. You may call me Yaya."

He bowed his head slightly in acknowledgment.

"Do you believe in fate?" she asked.

Tony shook his head. "No, ma'am. But I do believe in divine

guidance. I believe the Lord leads us places we need to be, when we need to be there."

"It is why your queen is still alive."

"Correct. She was sick when the car..."

Yaya waved a hand. "No. I read the papers, young man. I saw the stories about Henry Eit." She spit into the planter next to her chair. "No good, that man. I know this for many years. But, if the papers are to be believed, the only reason you were finally able to arrest him was because Duke Alexander overheard something he should not have, correct?"

"Yes, ma'am."

"Then you understand when I tell you I believe God brought you to the right taxi driver today."

Tony blinked slowly. "What do you mean?"

"Come. I show you." Yaya slowly stood. Tony reached for her to give her a hand, but she waved him off.

He followed her to the courtyard and toward a decorative door, covered with hanging plants. One of Yaya's wrinkled hands reached through the greenery and did something Tony couldn't see. The door swung open revealing a small room behind it. He looked at Yaya. "What is this?"

"This is the place Michaela and Nicklaus stayed when they fled Ravenzario."

Michelle Metcalf set her suitcase down next to her bed. It was good to be home.

"Michelle?" Nicholas's voice carried up the stairs. "Where do you want the rest of this stuff?"

"I don't care," she called back. "We'll deal with it later."

There was a thump followed by quick steps up the staircase.

Nicholas rounded the corner into her room. "You glad to be back, Mom?"

He'd been in her care for twenty years and had called her mom most of that time, but it never failed to both make her uneasy and fill her with love. It was good that he called her by name, too. It reminded her he wasn't really her son.

"The cruise was wonderful." She smiled as he flopped onto her bed. "Thank you for the gift."

"I'm just bummed we had to wait so long to take it. It was supposed to be a way to get out of the Midwest during the winter, not when it's almost summer."

Michelle shook her head and gave him a mock glare. "You had classes, exams, and none of the cruises we wanted to take coincided with your spring break. Waiting until the semester ended was perfect."

"I still can't believe you wouldn't let me get international texting on my phone while we were gone. I only sent Tessa three messages the whole time."

Nicholas had saved for two years to buy them the cruise, but household expenses, including cell phones, were paid by Michelle's job. The account filled with funds from King Richard prior to his death hadn't been touched in many years. Not since they'd fled Athmetis weeks after the assassination. The money had been used to purchase plane tickets to the United States. Some of it she later used to purchase their first home. King Richard's connections, including a couple of men whose names she still didn't know, had helped her secure what she needed but once the plane landed in the U.S., they had been on their own.

Deciding a single woman with a young son and no visible means of income would be suspicious, Michelle took the first job she could find. The daycare provided her with a place for Nicholas to be with her at all times, but still be around other children. For months he didn't even sleep in his own room for Michelle's peace of mind and because of the nightmares that continued to plague him. Her own sleep had often been less than restful with fears for Nicholas's safety always in the forefront of her mind. When she did doze off, she'd been hounded by dreams of her own.

The icy water. The king yelling at her to take Nicklaus and go. The fear of being found too soon. The fear of drowning. Of freezing as she tried to carry the terrified three-year-old to the safe house only she and the king knew about. The small, secret rooms in Ravenzario. The trail left to Athmetis. The short stay underground. Virtually no time outside of that little room for over a month. It had, quite literally, nearly driven her insane.

Michelle shook her head to clear it of the distant memories. Why were they suddenly in the forefront of her mind? "What?" she asked, dimly aware Nicholas had asked a question.

"I asked if you heard about the guy who used to live down in the Springfield, Missouri area?" He was used to her wool gathering, but he still seemed annoyed.

She hoisted the suitcase and set it on the bed next to him. "No, I don't believe I did."

"I heard some people talking about some rumors on the ship the day we boarded, but I forgot all about it until a minute ago." He tapped on his phone. "Yep. There's this guy from near Springfield who married some queen in Europe."

A feeling of dread filled Michelle's stomach. She'd carefully followed the goings on in Ravenzario and knew of the coincidence. What were the odds sweet Christiana would have married a man who lived less than four hours from her brother? She'd watched the wedding, even more astounded at the man chosen to walk the queen down the aisle. Michelle picked up one of the few remaining clean shirts and turned to put in her drawer. "I heard something about the wedding. Last fall, wasn't it?"

"Yeah. You watched part of it, didn't you?" He went on before she could answer. "But apparently, he got shot just a little over a week ago."

She couldn't turn around. He'd see it written all over her face. "What?"

"Uh..." He must be reading an article. "So this Alexander guy married the queen last fall. I guess her uncle was a bad dude who'd been arrested, but he was given some kind of Easter pardon."

A pardon? How had she missed that? She'd read about his arrest when it happened two years earlier and waited impatiently for someone to contact her, to tell her it was safe to finally return to her homeland, but no one ever did.

"He somehow got onto the palace grounds and tried to kill the queen. I guess she managed to get away."

Michelle silently cheered her former charge. She always had been an ingenious little girl. The pictures from after the accident nearly broke Michelle's heart.

"But Alexander - he's a duke now, I guess - was fighting this uncle and got shot in the leg. He's going to be okay and this time, the uncle was charged with treason."

Could it really be safe? He'd gone after Christiana again. She knew that, after nearly two decades running the country, he had to have far-reaching tentacles. The stories a few months earlier about Christiana's first fiancé proved that. The acquisition of an Easter pardon did so again. No. Until someone came to tell her it was safe, she wouldn't tell Nicholas the truth, and they wouldn't return. Until they *had* to.

"Mom?"

Nicholas caught her attention again and she turned. "What is it?"

Before she realized what was happening, he'd rolled off the bed and stood in front of her. "What's wrong, Mom?"

"What do you mean?"

He gently wiped the tears off one of her cheeks. "You're crying."

She managed to give him a small smile. "I suppose I am."

"Why?"

"I didn't want to tell you before the cruise, but I learned something recently." She hadn't known before the cruise, but she didn't want to tell him exactly when she'd received the information. "We've been safe here a long time, but it's time to start thinking about moving."

Nicholas crossed his arms in front of his chest. "What brought that up?"

"That comment you made about the pardon. I received word that one of the men who would like to harm us was pardoned not too long ago. I'd hoped to wait until I had more information to tell you, but that mention of it must have triggered something in me." She hated lying to him, but she couldn't tell him the whole truth. Not yet. She prayed he wouldn't pick up on her duplicity.

"So we're moving again?" He'd hate it, but he'd already resigned himself to the idea.

"I don't know yet." She reached for a Kleenex. "Let me do some research, and I'll let you know soon." The research would be more about where to go than if they would move. By the end of the month, they'd be settled somewhere new.

2

This time when Tony stepped off the airplane, he was greeted by southern humidity. He thought Baton Rouge was probably better than New Orleans, but what did he know? Yaya had passed on what information she had, which wasn't much. She hadn't known what last name they'd used, just that Michaela was now going by Michelle and Nicklaus became Nicholas. Of course, that had been nearly two decades earlier. Despite the lack of withdrawals from the account set up to help with expenses, it was possible they could have changed their names again or had a second set of identification papers ready that Yaya knew nothing about.

He'd prayed nonstop during the fairly short flight to Athmetica, and God had led him to exactly the person he needed to see. The trip to the United States had taken much longer, and he'd slept for much of it, but when he was awake Tony beseeched the Lord for the same favor here.

This time, he rented a car and drove himself to the town of Boaz, Louisiana. The sign proudly proclaimed it to be the friend-liest town for fifty miles, but it seemed like he hadn't seen a real town in at least that long. All five thousand residents must be super proud of their title.

Rather than checking into a hotel, Tony decided he'd visit the diner first. The silver, domed rectangular building fit every stereotype for a diner of its kind. He sat at the back booth facing the front door. After a couple of minutes, a waitress stopped by with a glass of water.

"What can I get ya to eat, mister?"

Tony glanced through the menu and only recognized a small portion of the dishes. "What do you recommend?"

"We're know for our Shrimp or Oyster Poboy or the Seafood Gumbo. Which one ya want?"

He smiled up at her. "Whichever you recommend and a cup of coffee when you have a minute." The mid-afternoon crowd appeared to consist of himself, two elderly ladies playing a card game, and a gentleman who had to be older than the hills themselves. It could either be incredibly easy or incredibly difficult to get information out of this group.

The waitress, Norma Jean, returned with his cup of coffee and set it in front of him. "So what're you doin' in our little town, mister? Just passin' through?"

Tony shook his head. "No, ma'am."

Before he could continue, the man at the counter guffawed. Tony had never heard such a sound before, but the cross between a dying goat's laughter and the sound of a donkey braying had to be a guffaw. "You hear that, Curly?"

A large, bald man looked out from the kitchen. "Hear what, Earl?"

"This guy called Norma Jean 'ma'am.'"

Curly just shook his head and went back to his work. Earl, though, twisted his barstool until he faced them. "So, city boy, whatcha doin' here in our town? Ya cain't be from around here."

"No, I'm not," Tony admitted. "I'm from a country in the

Mediterranean, and I'm looking for some family members who moved here a number of years ago."

"Ya oughta talk to Wilma. She knows ever'one who's lived in these parts since the beginning of the century."

Tony started to ask which century, but Earl stopped him.

"The *last* century that is."

Okay then. "Where can I find her?"

Earl called to one of the ladies across the room. "Jane, what day is it?"

Neither woman looked up from their card game. "It's Tuesday, Earl. Same as it was the last three times you asked."

"It's Tuesday, mister." As though that explained everything.

Norma Jean rolled her eyes Earl's direction. "Wilma is getting her hair done." She scolded the man on the barstool. "You know that, Earl. You dropped her off."

Earl's laughter was far closer to a true chuckle this time. "I know."

"Is there something one of us might be able to help you with until she gets back?"

Tony hesitated then pulled out the pictures. "I'm looking for these two. They likely would have moved to town early in the year 2000, maybe January or February." Yaya hadn't known how long the trip was supposed to take, just that they weren't doing anything as simple as his travel arrangements had been. "Her name is probably Michelle, and his is Nicholas."

Earl guffawed again. "Ya don't know their names and ya expect us to tell you where they are? If we even knows them."

"I hope so." Tony leaned forward. "They were being threatened by a relative of the child. It's taken nearly two decades, but they're finally safe, and it's my job to find them."

"I dunno, mister." Earl seemed wary of him. "How do we know yer not the man lookin' for them? Why would we help you if you were?"

"You can't know for certain," Tony admitted. "But if you check for recent news from Ravenzario, you'll know I'm right."

A pretty girl in her late teens or early twenties walked in. "Who's here, Mama?"

Norma Jean sighed and moved to greet her. After a long hug, she whispered something in the girl's ear before taking her apron off. The girl put it on and made her way around to each of the customers in the room. By the time she finished talking about some kind of apple pie bake off coming up, his food was ready.

"I'm Betty Sue," she told him topping off his coffee as she set the plate down. "Can I get ya anything else?"

Tony decided one more risk was worth taking. He set the photos on the table. "I'm looking for Michelle and Nick."

Betty Sue narrowed her eyes and studied the pictures. "I'm pretty sure that's Nick Metcalf. I ran into them in Florida a couple weeks ago. They're up near St. Louis now, I think. On the Illinois side, but I'm not sure what town."

Rather than waiting to see if the food was as good as everyone said, Tony dropped a twenty on the table and left the room, questions streaming in his wake. Less than two weeks earlier, they'd lived in St. Louis.

He had to be getting close.

Michelle spent the next day trying to figure out where would be the best place to run and how to get there. When she and King Richard plotted how to get away and had written up the plan, they'd agreed on a list of cities. There were about twenty on the list and she'd lived in five since the accident. This time, she wanted somewhere else. Though the king had assured her the plans were well hidden, and no one without certain specific knowledge of palace hiding places would be able to find them, she couldn't be sure they hadn't fallen into the wrong hands. After all, Henry had been in power for a very long time.

"What're you doing?" Nicholas flopped down into the big chair across from her.

"Trying to decide where we're going to go if we have to move." Some place off the beaten path would be good.

"Do we really have to?" Even though he was an adult, Nicholas could whine with the best of them when he didn't want to do something.

"I'm not sure yet." She was, but no sense in upsetting him until it was time.

"I have a date this weekend."

And there it was. Something she'd worked very hard to avoid. For many years, Michelle had used the fear of whoever was chasing them as a way to keep Nicholas from dating, though she'd never told him he was engaged and had been since he was three-years-old.

"And what about our trip to Europe? We've already got tickets flying out of here."

The cruise had been his gift to her. Her gift to him was a trip to Europe. Specifically, a trip to Ravenzario or Mevendia for his wedding. She'd refused to think about what would happen if he declined to marry Princess Yvette. Since he was little, she'd tried to prepare him as much as she could without flat out telling him. There were pictures of Yvette around the house and always had been. When he'd asked who she was, Michelle told him she was the daughter of his birth father's best friend and that their fathers had hoped they would marry someday. Nicholas had looked forward to meeting her eventually, when it was safe. Over the last couple of years, he'd started to chafe more and more at the idea and wanted to date the girls he already knew.

Finally, she said, "You know how I feel about you dating. And we can change the tickets." It would cost money, but she would do it. His safety was paramount.

13

"Yeah. You and my biological father, who I don't remember even a little bit, wanted me to end up with his best friend's daughter, Eve. I get that. But I've never met her. I'm sure she's a lovely girl, but I want to find someone *I* like, not someone somebody else picked for me."

Even more reason to pick up and move soon. Cut his attachment to the girls in his life here in Edwardsville. There had been more than one fight over allowing him to have social media accounts during his teen years. She'd refused, and he still didn't have any, so he wouldn't be able to keep up with anyone that way. If she had to, she'd "accidentally" drop his phone in a sink full of sudsy water and discover it wasn't backed up to her computer. No phone numbers to text then. Closing her eyes, she breathed a prayer for patience and protection. "I need you to pack a go bag. It's been a while since we updated them."

If they left - *when* they left - they wouldn't pack the house or take anything with them except what they could carry in a suitcase or two. They'd have to find a new life somewhere else and start over. The cash she had squirreled away ever since their arrival would go with them and help them get set up.

With a glare, Nicholas headed for the stairs, hopefully to pack. She needed to do the same, to decide what to take with her. She packed only a few outfits and filled most of her suitcase with knick knacks and mementos. Christmas ornaments he'd made in preschool. Pictures from his first baseball game. The framed photos of Yvette. From the safe, she pulled a fireproof box big enough to hold the paperwork she'd need to prove they were who she said they were. And something else Nicholas had only seen once. He'd need it for his wedding. She wouldn't give it to him until they returned to Ravenzario. Another layer of clothes, including her dress for the wedding, went over the top of everything.

"I'm packed." Nicholas's sullen voice drifted down the hallway. "Can I leave now?"

"No." She didn't want him going anywhere. They still only had one car, and she needed it here. One last picture. She picked it up as tears filled her eyes.

"What is it?" The tender side of Nicholas must have surfaced when he saw her looking at the picture of the two of them taken not long after they fled.

"Just praying you stay safe." Her fingers traced his chubby three-year-old cheek. She could see the traces of fear in her own eyes, but Nicholas had already forgotten those fears - at least during the daytime. He was laughing the full-bodied laugh she'd always loved.

He wrapped an arm around her shoulders. "I'm safe, Mom. Whoever it is that's out to get me has forgotten about us a long time ago."

Michelle shook her head. "I know you think that, and I can understand why. Someday soon I'll tell you the whole story, and then you'll see why the people who chased us are still out there."

"Why don't you tell me the whole story now?"

She thought about that. Turned it over in her mind. She'd planned to wait until they were already in Europe, but maybe things had changed. Before she could make up her mind, her phone beeped, letting her know she had a text message. After swiping the tears from her face, she picked it up and knew this was an answer to prayer. A plea from a friend, entreating her to visit.

Not yet, but when they did leave in the next few days, that's where they'd go. No one would think to look for them there. She'd just have to pull up directions on her computer because her phone may not be able to find the small town.

Before she could text back, the ringtone sounded and a name from their Louisiana days appeared on the screen.

"Norma Jean?" Nicholas asked. "What's she want?"

Michelle didn't answer him, but swiped the phone. "Hello?"

Norma Jean didn't exchange pleasantries. "Remember how you told me someone was after y'all?"

With her stomach turning into a lead ball, Michelle answered. "Yes. You promised you'd let me know if anyone showed up looking for us."

"He was here a few hours ago. Me an' Earl didn't tell him nothin', but Betty Sue didn't get the memo. I tried to tell her, but she didn't understan'. He knows you're livin' in Illinois outside St. Louie. I don't know what kinda plan you got for hightailin' it outta there, but I think you'd best do it and fast."

Michelle thanked her and hung up.

"What'd Ms. Norma Jean say?"

She looked up to see fear beginning to take hold in Nicholas's eyes. She couldn't bear to tell him, but she had no choice.

"It's time to go, isn't it?" Instead of the anger she feared, his voice held only resignation. "I'll get the suitcases. You grab whatever else we need."

While Nicholas loaded the car, Michelle found the map she needed and printed it off. For good measure, she printed off nearly a dozen others to small towns and big cities alike, pre-chosen for their randomness. They couldn't take the computer, or their nosy neighbors would know they were leaving for good. This was the best she could do to lay down a false trail.

Nicholas called up the stairs. "All packed!"

She looked around the room one last time. They'd both loved it here, but it was time to do what she had to do to keep her prince safe. "God protect us," she whispered and shut off the light.

Time to go.

3

Tony sat on a bench at a small park near the house he believed to be Michelle and Nicholas's current home. The park was only a couple of lots without houses built on them. Instead, it was home to a small pond and, currently, a few ducks. He brought a full loaf of bread with him to give him an excuse to stay there for a while without calling too much attention to himself. He hoped.

He sat there for hours, and there was no movement at the house. No cars. No lights turned on. Nothing.

By the time dusk settled in, he knew he couldn't sit there much longer. He found a spot where he could observe a bit more surreptitiously and parked his car in such a way that he could see the back of the house. He stayed awake as long as he could but dozed a few times before the sun rose. He drove back to the park and sat on the bench again. This time there were no ducks to feed and, two hours in, an elderly woman wandered in and sat on the next bench over.

"I love days like this," she said after a few minutes. "I do miss the ducks though."

"The ducks are nice, when you have something to feed them," Tony agreed.

"You are the man who was here yesterday, then."

He couldn't hide it. She already knew he'd been there. "Yes."

"Why?"

"I'm waiting for someone." The truth.

"In a neighborhood park?"

He nodded, but didn't answer.

"Michelle and Nicholas left on another trip yesterday morning."

Tony blinked. "Pardon?"

"You are watching their house, yes?" Her light blue eyes seemed to bore right through him.

"I'm waiting for some old friends. I was told they live in this neighborhood."

"I see." She stood and glared at him. "If you're still here in an hour, I will call the police." With that, she straightened, turned, and walked away.

Tony's eyes narrowed as he watched her. So she'd pretended to be much more infirm than she really was. Interesting. But he'd learned what he needed to. Come dark, he'd see if he could get into their house and find any indication where they'd gone.

To that end, he spent the rest of his day pouring over maps at his hotel, trying to discover what he could about the neighborhood and the best way to approach the house without raising suspicions.

He also communicated several times with Prince Alexander. The queen didn't know why Tony had taken several weeks off. Only Alexander, who Tony trusted implicitly, knew of his search for the young prince. Alexander put Tony in touch with a friend of his from Serenity Landing, some four hours away. Jonathan Langley-Cranston promised to send one of his best men to help Tony both get into the house and to find anything left to be found.

Darkness fell again, and he traveled with Karl to a spot a few blocks away. From there, they made their way to the house and in just a few seconds, Karl had the door unlocked. Inside, Tony simply observed for the first several minutes. Several empty nails on the walls showed where pictures had been recently removed. A few others remained, but they were mainly decorative in nature.

"Sir?" Karl called from upstairs. "I found the computer."

Tony met him in a spare-bedroom-turned-office. "Can you get into it?"

"Probably." It went through the boot up process. Tony sucked in a breath when the background picture appeared. "What is it?" Karl asked.

"I presume that's Michelle and Nicholas. I haven't seen them in nearly twenty years, but that looks like her." He held up the photo he'd brought with him. "Don't you think?"

"I do."

A tall young man had his arm around Michelle's shoulders. An emerald green cap and gown, along with the year emblazoned on the stole hanging around his neck, seemed to indicate a high school graduation several years earlier. The prince had grown into a handsome young man.

Karl shook his head and made a tsking sound. "No password."

In a few minutes, the printer was humming with the data Michelle had recently looked up, including maps to a number of towns across the country. While he waited to look through it all, Tony searched the rest of the upstairs. Nicholas's room was nice. Orderly, but not overly so. A few pictures of him with friends still remained. His drawers and closet weren't empty. Neither were Michelle's when Tony went in there. A safe stood in her closet, open and emptied.

Karl walked in, a sheaf of papers in his hand and spread them across the queen bed in Michelle's room. "Where do you think they're headed next?"

Tony shrugged. "Some of these towns are on the list of places they came up with before the accident. The rest are not. I'm not convinced she'd go to one of those. If she believed the prince was in danger, she may have deviated from the plan written nearly two decades ago."

"Quite true. Based on her searches, I'd say these three are your best bets." Karl separated three sets of information from the others. "Phoenix, Arizona is the first one. It's on the list, but it's *hot*. She may have decided not to go there because of the heat."

"Or she may have decided no one would believe they would go there for the same reason. Plus it's big enough to get lost in." Tony ran a hand through his hair. A variation of the same answer could be given for all of the locations. The others weren't on the list, and Tony's gut told him she'd picked a location no one could connect to her. "Can we get access to her phone records?"

"Maybe." They went back to the other room, and Karl clicked a few things in the open browser. "Yep. Her passwords were saved in the browser." A few seconds later, the printer hummed again. "I've printed off all the ones I can access."

Tony was most interested in the recent calls or texts. If they'd left forty-eight hours earlier, then... He found several text messages and phone calls to long distance numbers with the same area code. "Where's this phone from?"

Karl looked at it. "I think that's a Minnesota number." He tapped it into the search engine on his phone rather than opening a new tab on the computer. "Yes. It's from Mallard Lake Township." A couple more taps on his phone, and he handed it to Tony. "One seems to be the hard line connected to the local bakery."

"Well then, we know where I'm going next." Mallard Lake Township, Minnesota. Would he find them there? He prayed he could. They needed to bring the prince back and soon.

Michelle collapsed onto the bed at Mallard Lake Inn. Two

days of driving nearly non-stop. Forty-eight hours to make a twelve-hour drive. They'd started by going east, then south a bit, west, south some more, north somewhat, east, back roads, further west, northwest, and finally figured out the most direct route to Mallard Lake Township from Cheyenne, while still avoiding main roads at all costs. To follow them, this man would have to have Iron Man's resources or possibly Bruce Wayne's.

She shook her head. Nicholas had been fascinated with the comic book superheroes as a child. He'd always identified with Superman, though she'd never told him the truth. Sent away from a dying planet. The sole survivor. The comparison wasn't perfect, of course, but there were definite similarities.

"Mom?" Nicholas came out of the bathroom. "Are you ready to talk about this?"

She sat up, cross-legged on the bed. "Have a seat. I told you I'd tell you more when we got here." Michelle pulled her picture sleeves out of her purse and stared at the first one she and Nicholas had taken to establish their cover. Once they'd settled down, she'd never made it a secret she wasn't his biological mother, though everyone believed her to be his aunt.

Nicholas pulled the office chair out from the desk and stretched his long legs until his feet were crossed on the foot of her bed. "So who's the bad guy after me?"

Michelle took in a deep breath and blew it out slowly. "Your father was a very powerful man in your area. Your mother's half-brother detested him to the point of trying to kill your entire family."

Nicholas's expression didn't change except for a few seconds of rapid blinking. "So Uncle Evil decided to kill me and my parents because he didn't like my dad?"

Michelle stared at the picture, unable to look directly at him. "He also planned to kill your sister and take over everything himself."

The silence lasted long minutes this time. "I have a sister?" Nicholas finally asked.

"Yes."

"Is she still alive? Or did he kill her, too?"

"She's still alive."

He bolted out of his chair. "She's alive, and I've never met her? She's never come to look for me?"

"Please sit down."

"No."

"Nicholas." She spoke more sharply than she meant. "Sit down." But it did the job.

He sank back into the chair.

"Your sister is only a couple years older than you. You, your parents, and I were in the car driving through some mountains two days before Christmas 1999. Your sister was ill, or she would have been with you instead of me, your nanny. There was only room for four in that car. I would have been in another vehicle close behind." With the security teams and other staff. She closed her eyes and prayed for strength.

"The car went over a cliff and landed in a river below. Your parents were severely injured. You and I were both hurt, but not as badly. Your father had blood streaming down his face, but he was conscious. He told me to take you and run. We'd had a plan in place should something happen, so I got you out of your seat and walked through the river until I was a safe distance away and could climb out with you while not leaving much of a trail."

"That doesn't explain why no one came for me."

"It's not that simple. You were to have inherited everything, despite your sister being older. With you gone, she did, but she was only five. The security around her was increased significantly, and your uncle ran things on her behalf for many years. He must have decided it was close enough. I heard he was arrested a few years ago, but instructions had been left for someone to contact us. They never did. I assumed the danger hadn't passed. Just in the last few weeks, I heard he was no longer in prison. I have no specific reason to believe he'll be looking for us, but when Norma Jean said someone had old pictures, who else could it be?"

"But you're still not going to tell me who it is so I can look it all up for myself?"

Michelle shook her head. "Not yet. And I have no idea if your sister knows for certain neither of us died. I have reason to believe she's always been told all four of us were killed." She hesitated before going on. "There are graves with our names on them near those of your parents."

He was understandably skeptical. "So I could Google the grave of Nicholas Metcalf and find my own grave?"

"No. Your given name is not Nicholas Metcalf, and mine is not Michelle. Before you ask, no, I won't tell you what they are."

"Why didn't you tell me all of this sooner?" Nicholas ran both hands through his dark hair. "I could have handled the truth."

"The last few years, you could have, but when you were a child? Should I have told you when you were five? Eight? How old? You've always been safer not knowing."

"Then why are we running again? We've never run like this before."

Every place they'd lived had a secure location for him to run to if she used a particular code word, and he was never to consider the coast clear unless she used another one. There had always been a "go bag" at the ready, but every other time they'd moved, there had been boxes and a moving truck and an actual *move*, though she'd never let him know ahead of time where they were going.

He was right. This time was different. They'd packed their go bags and left.

"Someone was in Boaz looking for us. Until I know who it is, it's not safe."

Nicholas leaned forward, resting his forearms on his knees. "Michelle, you've been the only mother I've ever known. I love you for taking care of me all these years, but at some point, we're both going to have to realize that I'm not a child anymore. You'll need to tell me the whole truth and let me learn to take care of myself."

She knew the day was coming. It didn't mean she was looking forward to it.

"After Europe," she finally told him, hoping he would think she was simply stalling for time. "After the trip to Europe, I'll answer any questions you have."

4

Tony caught a flight to Minneapolis-St. Paul from St. Louis and rented another car. Mallard Lake Township wasn't large, and he didn't want to arrive in the middle of the night, so he stopped in St. Cloud about two hours away for a good night's sleep. He made it to Mallard Lake by mid-morning.

Driving every road in the entire town didn't take long. His research said only about 2500 people lived there, but it was the closest town of any size to the popular Mallard Lake Resort and Recreation Area just two miles away. Though a couple of resorts and numerous other water and ski related businesses were on the lake, visitors would come to Mallard Lake Township to shop for groceries and for things they'd forgotten or gifts to take back to their loved ones.

He'd made reservations at one of the nicer resorts on the lake itself. Michelle and Nicholas wouldn't stay at such a popular place, but it would be an excellent base of operations. By eleven, he had parked his car in a public lot on one end of the historic downtown district. Stores of all kinds lined the street. A cafe, an antique shop, a quilt store, a swim and ski shop. He doubted they sold both kinds of goods at the same time.

The old fashioned fire and police stations drew his eye, and a sign explained the daily tour of both, including the historical museum and other parts of town with historical significance. Maybe he'd do that another day.

Once he passed Main Street, he found the bakery Karl had told him about. Across the street was a bar and grill, still closed for the afternoon. He doubted things got too crazy very often. It just didn't seem like that kind of town. Two churches stood on opposite sides of the street from each other. The parking lots weren't large, but he hoped their services didn't start or stop at the same time. The traffic jam would be annoying for everyone.

After spending what he considered to be an acceptable amount of time wandering around the stores in general, he went into the bakery. The smell of cakes, chocolate, and every other kind of deliciousness met him as he walked in.

"Hi! Welcome to Millie's Bakery!" A woman who looked to be in her mid-twenties welcomed him.

"Hello." He smiled back. "Are you Millie?"

She laughed. "No. Millie was my grandmother. She passed not too long ago and left this place to me. I'm Brianna. Are you new in town?"

"You could say that. A friend of mine came to visit not too long ago and loved it here. I had some time off and decided to check it out."

She cocked her head. "Where are you from? I don't recognize the accent."

"Oh here and there." Best to be vague. "You're likely hearing a hodge podge of accents." Hodge podge was a phrase he'd picked up in Louisiana.

"That's probably it then. What can I get for you today?"

He looked at the delectable concoctions in the display case. "What do you recommend?"

"Our seasonal specialty is this cupcake. Chocolate chip with chocolate frosting."

Tony nodded. "I'll take one." After paying her and accepting a cup of coffee, Tony sat at one of the small tables with a view of the whole place. He wanted to ask her if she knew Michelle and Nicholas, but something held him back.

His dessert-for-lunch was half gone when the door opened again. The woman who walked in made Tony want to sit up and pay more attention, but he forced himself to remain calm.

"Michelle!" Brianna exclaimed as she hurried around the counter. "I'm so glad you're here!"

So apparently, Tony had beat Michelle and Nicholas to Mallard Lake Township, if her friend's reaction was any indication.

"I'm glad I made it." Michelle returned the woman's hug. "Your invitation couldn't have come at a better time."

Brianna looked concerned. "What's going on? Something..."

Michelle cut her off. "Nothing specific, just a good time for us to get out of town, that's all."

"Well, I'm glad you're here. You always were a better people person than I am. I've managed to keep going so far, but I need help! Between running the shop and trying to sort through all of Granny's things in the evenings, it's just been too much."

"I'm glad I can help. What can I do?"

Brianna nodded toward Tony who'd only been watching out of the corner of his eye. "This gentleman needs some more coffee to go with the rest of his cupcake. Then I'll teach you how to work the register, so you can help me during the lunch rush."

Tony could hardly believe his luck. Even as he thought it, he knew luck had nothing to do with it, and he thanked God for leading him to the right place.

Michelle took the coffee pot from Brianna and filled his cup.

"Thank you," he said, looking her straight in the eyes. They'd never met before, but would she somehow know?

"My pleasure." Michelle smiled right at him. "Is there anything else I can get for you?"

Tony chuckled. "Somehow I doubt you have any more idea than I do when it comes to finding something in here."

She grinned back at him. "You have a good point. But if there's something you need, I'd be happy to figure it out."

"No. I'm good, but thank you." He held out a hand. "I'm Anthony. It seems I've been in town about as long as you have."

She shook it. "Michelle. We seem to be Mallard Lake Township's newest residents."

"Alas, I am not a resident, merely a visitor to one of the resorts, but I will be here for a while." He looked around. "My employer informed me I had way too much vacation time built up and if I didn't take it, I'd lose it." Close enough to the truth. He rarely took vacation days, knowing Henry could try something at any time. "Perhaps you and I could explore Mallard Landing Township together?" Was he asking her on a date? He hadn't intended to, but he suddenly found himself praying she'd say yes and not just because she was the protector of Prince Nicklaus.

Suddenly, he was much more interested in getting to know the woman who had given her entire life to protect her charge.

Was this guy asking her out? She hadn't been on a real date since before she'd been chosen as the nanny for Princess Christiana and Crown Prince Nicklaus so many years earlier. It wasn't forbidden while she worked for the royal family, but it would have been difficult for many reasons. For several years, she was too busy looking over her shoulder for monsters to come out of the shadows. As Nicholas grew, she made a conscious choice not to date.

But Nicholas's words from the night before came back to her. He was an adult. Before long, he would be married to Princess Yvette, and she would slip quietly back into the night. Perhaps return to her quiet life in the United States, not much more than a footnote in the story of his long exile. This time she'd be able to stay in touch with her family, go back to visit them sometimes.

The mere thought made her heart hurt, but she knew it would be best. And here and now, this man was waiting for an answer. She nodded. "That would be lovely." Perhaps when she returned, after delivering Prince Nicklaus to his sister and his bride, she would have someone waiting for her.

"When do you get off work?" His eyes twinkled at her, and she knew he was teasing.

She laughed with him. "I have no idea. The shop closes at..." She squinted to read the backwards writing on the door. "Eight. I'd imagine no later than 8:30 then, but I really don't know."

A voice called from the kitchen. "You can go play tourist once the lunch rush is over. As long as you promise to be back by dinner."

Anthony smiled. "After lunch then?"

The door opened and they both looked to see who came in. Nicholas. Just what she needed. He wouldn't like the idea of her dating.

"Mom, can I get the keys to the car from you? I think mine are in my bag." He didn't even look at the patron sitting next to her. Michelle hadn't raised him to be rude. When he resumed his life as a prince, he would need to be unfailingly polite.

"Nicholas." She knew there was a bit of reproach in her voice, and he looked around in response.

He turned his best grin on Anthony. "My apologies, sir. See, my mother has the keys to the car, and my phone is in there." Nicholas winked at Michelle. "I'm sure you can appreciate my anxiety."

Michelle hid her wince, knowing her white lie would irritate him. "It's not in there. I grabbed it for you, but I dropped it. The screen shattered beyond repair." When she stepped on it with the heel of her boot. "I'll see if we can find someone to fix it or get you a new one in the next couple of days."

As she expected, Nicholas frowned at her. "For real?" She watched him take a deep breath and let it out slowly, just like she'd taught him. "It's okay. I know you wouldn't do it on purpose."

Her conscience pricked her, but it was for the greater good. "I'm sorry." *I'm sorry it was necessary*, she added to herself.

"Well, in that case, I saw a couple of help wanted signs on my walk over. I'll give them your phone number if they need one."

"That's fine." He wouldn't need a job soon. If she'd tap into the funds left for her to take care of him, neither one of them would need to work, but at the same time she was glad he'd learned a good work ethic.

He put an arm around her shoulder and gave her a quick hug. "I'll be back later."

Michelle watched him walk out before turning back to Anthony.

"Your son?" he asked taking a sip of his coffee.

"My nephew. I've raised him since his parents died when he was very young. I never legally adopted him, though."

"He loves you."

She turned to look at the door Nicholas had walked through. "He does. He always has. I don't know what I'll do without him." Her eyes misted.

"What you'll do without him? Is he going somewhere?" Anthony snapped her out of it.

She brushed one hand down her shirt, tugging on the hem. "Don't all children grow up and leave to one extent or another?"

"I suppose they do."

Michelle took a deep breath and looked back at Anthony. "Is there anything else you need at the moment?"

"Nope. I'm good." He smiled at her, and she could feel the blush rising in her face. "Can I get your number in case something comes up between now and the end of the lunch rush?"

The bell over the door rang again, giving her an out. "Just meet me here later?"

He smiled again. "Sure."

Michelle hurried behind the counter as Brianna came out of the kitchen. For the next fifteen minutes, Brianna showed her everything she needed to know about running the front counter. The cold sandwiches were brought in from a sandwich shop two towns over so there was no way to prepare them for each customer. Several, with names written on them, were set aside as prior orders. Many of them, she learned, were regulars she would get to know. The register was easy to use. The pricing structure was simple, which helped.

By the time noon hit, she had become familiar with most of the items and knew she couldn't sample regularly, not if she had any prayer of fitting into the dress she'd purchased for Nicholas's wedding. She *had* brought that with her though it would need to be pressed before she wore it.

Brianna came out of the kitchen again. Michelle knew she'd been working non-stop back there. "That's it," she said, leaning against the counter. "The next couple hours will be slow. I can't begin to thank you for your help."

Michelle just smiled. "It was my pleasure, really. I enjoyed myself."

"Remember that a couple months from now when you're ready to throw a cupcake at someone."

Michelle gasped. "I would *never* throw a cupcake at anyone!"

They laughed together, and Brianna wiped down the counter. "Would you mind straightening up in the dining area and then you can go explore with that guy?"

"Not a problem." She prayed the dining room wouldn't be too bad, but the way the shop was set up, she really couldn't see it very well. She walked around the counter to see Anthony wiping down a table before throwing a napkin in the trash.

He turned to look at her. "Ready to go?"

5

Tony still wasn't sure what had compelled him to ask her out or to keep the dining area clean while she worked during the rush, but he was glad he had.

The image of Prince Nicklaus stuck with him and had replayed in his mind for the last two hours. The prince was looking for a job. On one level, Tony understood the rationale behind making sure he had a good work ethic, but at the same time, it didn't quite sit right for the Crown Prince to be working.

And that was something else they hadn't addressed. Alexander told him to worry about it later.

Nicklaus should be the monarch, not Christiana.

When Nicklaus's continued existence became public, they would have to deal with that. If he wanted to, he could force Christiana to give up her throne. It wouldn't be *easy*, but Nicklaus could if he wanted to. Tony knew Christiana was the right one to lead Ravenzario during the current difficulties, coming out of the betrayals by her uncle and later her fiancé. But Nicklaus had the birthright and as the rightful heir could force her out, though it wouldn't be easy. The rift it would cause among the Ravenzarian people could be worse than anything they'd seen in the last few years.

He shook himself out of his stupor. "Is there anything in particular we need to see?" he asked Michelle.

"I have no idea. I've never been here before." She smiled up at him, almost as though she expected him to know.

"I haven't either. Should we ask Brianna?"

Michelle glanced toward the counter then shook her head. "How about we start with a walking tour of the historic downtown area?"

"Good idea." He held open the door for her. "I noticed they do tours. Want to see if we can get one?"

She tilted her head as she thought about it. "Not today. I feel more like just kind of wandering."

"Then wander we shall." They started down Main Street walking next to each other but not touching. "Is there any store you'd particularly like to see?" He pointed to one storefront. "Do you need a new quilt?"

She seemed to hesitate. "You know, I think I would like to commission a quilt. I wonder if they do that sort of thing."

Tony looked both directions before starting across the street. "If they don't, I would imagine they know someone who does."

The shop had a bell above the door, and it jangled as they walked in. Tony didn't know much about quilts, but he knew these were high quality. Perhaps he should have one made for the new little prince or princess to arrive later in the year.

"Hello," a young woman with light blond hair said as she walked out from the back. "How can I help you?"

"I think we're just looking right now," Michelle told her. "Do you create custom pieces?"

The woman nodded. "I do. If you can give me an idea of what you'd like, I can sketch out a design and discuss price with you."

Michelle ran a hand over one in front of her. "These are lovely."

"Thank you." Her eyes twinkled as she spoke. "That one is a double wedding ring quilt."

Michelle pulled her hand back as though she'd been burned. "I would like to talk to you about a custom one." She glanced at Tony. "Not right now, but soon." What was that about? "How long does it take to have one made?"

"It depends."

Tony didn't tune them out, but he did move away as they talked. He rubbed one of the quilts between his fingers. Obviously high quality. The stitching was nearly, but not quite, perfect, indicating it had been hand stitched by someone who knew what she was doing. At least that's what he imagined it meant. They would hold up quite well, which is what one wanted in a quilt for a baby, wasn't it?

What kind of quilt did Michelle want? And why had she reacted so strongly to the wedding quilt?

The women finished talking for the moment, and Tony jumped in. "I would like to commission a quilt."

"Of course, sir. What do you have in mind?" She stood there with a notepad in her hand.

"My employers are having their first child in September. I've worked for their family since I was fifteen." He hadn't started in the security department, but had moved the minute he was old enough to begin training. To this day, he had no idea what possessed the king to promote him to head of security in his early twenties. Perhaps the king knew something everyone else didn't. Like Tony could be trusted.

That could be. How many members of security had been discovered to have connections to Henry? Including many who had been there longer than Tony.

"Do they know the gender of the child?" the proprietor asked.

He shook his head. "No. They have decided not to find out, but I do have some photos on my laptop that could serve as inspiration. Perhaps I can return later?" The colors of the Ravanzarian royal crest would need to be included, regardless of gender. He couldn't very well show her in front of Michelle though.

The woman showed him several of her completed quilts. He would come by without Michelle in the next day or two to finalize the design.

"You could email me the photos if you'd like."

He took the business card she offered. "If I email you today, when can we meet?"

They set up a time during lunch later in the week, and Michelle said she would stop by soon.

He held the door as they left, following Michelle as she turned to the left. Something seemed to be bothering her, but he couldn't figure out what it was.

Until it hit him.

She *knew* Nicklaus was supposed to be getting married in June. Two weeks after his twenty-first birthday. A week after Yvette's eighteenth. Except for a few last minute details, the wedding was planned.

Tony had been in charge of the security planning because it was the royal family, and it would take place on the same Bayfield property where Queen Christiana had married Duke Alexander. Not in Mevendia, though Princess Yvette had tried her best to move a wedding she believed would never happen. Why should she travel all the way to Ravenzario to be left at the altar?

Perhaps Michelle was feeling some of the same, wondering what her purpose in Ravenzario would be. He had no reason to believe she planned to let the date go by without somehow getting Nicklaus to his wedding. He also needed to return to the shop and commission a wedding quilt to give to the newlyweds, unless that was what Michelle planned.

"Are you all right?" he finally asked.

She stopped and he could see the moisture in her eyes. "I'm fine. My son is growing up."

"I understand."

"You have children?"

Tony shook his head. "No, but I have a young lady and a young man who I have been charged with seeing safely to adulthood. Neither one lives with me, or ever has, but I understand some of what you're feeling and I promise, it will be okay."

Michelle walked back into the bakery a few minutes after four. After Anthony commented about the children he'd been tasked with seeing to adulthood, they'd steered the conversation back in much safer directions. She needed to call Sophia and commission a quilt for Nicholas. It would be made from some of her favorite things that reminded her of him.

A few outfits from his childhood had been left in the care of Norma Jean. She would ship them. Assorted colors reminding him of different vacations they'd taken or his high school graduation. She probably should ask Sophia to make a wedding quilt for Nicholas and Princess Yvette, but to do so would make it all too real. For now, she could pretend the day would never come.

Maybe she could somehow get a hold of someone in Ravenzario and send Nicholas to Europe by himself with instructions to visit a particular person, who would make sure he had a good time. Would she be able to watch him walk down the aisle? As "the help" she would be relegated to a seat in the back of the Cathedral. Queen Christiana and her husband would fill the seats of Nicholas's family.

Despite her claims to the contrary, Michelle had never been family.

"What's wrong?"

How many people would ask her that today? Michelle just smiled at Brianna. "Just thinking. What do you need me to do?"

"Hey now! None of that! I want to know how it went with Mr. Cutie!"

"Anthony?"

Brianna raised an eyebrow. "Who else did you spend the afternoon with?"

"No one. We went to the quilt shop. I think I'm going to have Sophia make one for me. Do you know if her prices are reasonable for commissioned work?"

"I have no idea, but I can't imagine they'd be outrageous. I'm sure they're commensurate with the quality of the work, which is excellent."

Michelle nodded. "Of course. Now what do we need to do here?"

Brianna sighed. "Get ready for dessert. We don't sell dinner unless we happen to have some sandwiches left from lunch, which we don't. Generally, folks eat dinner elsewhere then come here for dessert."

"I can handle that. Why don't you go take a break and get dinner yourself?"

Brianna thought for a few seconds then nodded. "Where are you staying?"

Michelle told her where they'd spent the night before.

"Nope. Not gonna do it. I can't pay you much, but my grandmother left me her house, too. There's an apartment in this building. I insist you and Nicholas stay in one of them. I don't much care which one."

"Where have you been staying?" It would be an answer to prayer.

"I've been living in the apartment here, but either one is fine for me right now. Most of what I've been doing is business stuff first. I'll deal with the house once all of this is sorted and under control."

"In that case, we would be most grateful to stay in the house." A huge weight lifted off Michelle's shoulders. She no longer had to find a place to live in the next few days.

The rest of the evening passed uneventfully. Anthony didn't return. Nicholas stopped by for a minute to ask her something else, but got the car keys so he could take their bags to the house.

The next day started much the same, though without Anthony. She stopped by the quilt store during the afternoon lull. She and Sophia decided on a design and the seamstress would start on what she could until the box of clothes arrived from Norma Jean in a few days. It should be done before they left for Europe.

It wasn't until they began to close down the shop for the evening that Michelle realized what was missing. They'd only spent a couple of fairly superficial hours together the day before, but she found herself wishing Anthony had stopped in.

Brianna shooed Michelle out the door and locked it behind her. The walk to her new home wasn't far, but the sight she found when she turned the corner made her smile.

Anthony leaned against a light pole with an orchid in his hand. He held it out to her. "Good evening, Michelle."

"Hello, Anthony." Immediately somewhat suspicious, she warily took it from him. "What's this for?"

He shrugged and fell into step beside her. "I felt like we got off to a bad start yesterday. Or not *bad*," he hurried on, "but a bit weird. I think we both had a lot on our minds, and I'd like the chance to make it up to you."

Michelle twirled the flower between her fingers. "Thank you. I would enjoy that."

"Then dinner? Tomorrow?" He walked with his hands clasped behind his back. The day before he'd worn a jacket, but this evening the collared shirt showed off well-muscled but not overly large arms. He looked to be strong, but not showy. She liked that. She'd also liked the bit of spark that jumped between them when his fingers brushed hers as he handed off the flower.

It caught her off guard. Had she ever felt a spark like that? She knew the answer. Was she actually considering a *real date* with this man?

When he spoke, she realized how long it had been since he asked. At least a block. "It's okay." He smiled at her. "I'll just stop in for lunch tomorrow instead."

"No!" She surprised herself with her intensity. "I would love to have dinner with you, but I'll have to check with Brianna to see what night she doesn't need me to work."

Anthony gave her a half-smile. "Leave that to me. I'll make sure we can go tomorrow night, if that's what you want."

"You'll make sure? How are you planning to do that?" He wasn't a hit man was he? Surely, if he was, she and Nicholas would both be dead by now. What brought on those thoughts? The need to disappear after the call from Norma Jean? The upcoming trip to their homeland?

They stopped in front of the house, and Anthony winked at her. "Trust me."

It had been so long since she'd really trusted anyone, but Michelle found herself wanting to believe him. She nodded. "Okay. I trust you." She just prayed that trust wasn't misplaced.

6

"Anthony, right?"

Tony looked up from his meal to see Prince Nicklaus standing next to him. He held out a hand. "Yep. And you're Nick?" He couldn't imagine being so informal under any other circumstances. He still needed to find a way to get a DNA sample and send it to Alexander. Could this be his chance? He put the paperwork he'd been looking through back into his satchel.

"Nicholas," the prince replied, reminding Tony of the slight difference in his name. "Do you mind if I join you?"

Tony motioned to the seat across the café table from him. "Please do. Can I get you something to eat?"

Nicholas shook his head. "I already ate."

"I see." Tony held up a glass of water. "I decided on coffee after they brought this. You're welcome to it if you're thirsty. What can I help you with?" Was he going to tell Tony to back off? To stop seeing Michelle?

The young man turned out to be quite direct. "You asked my mom out."

"Yes," Tony answered slowly. "I suppose I did. Is that okay with you?"

Nicholas leaned forward, his forearms resting on the table. "She's everything I have in this world. If you hurt her, you answer to me."

Oh, how true that was! And he didn't even know it. "I have no intention of hurting her," Tony reassured him. "I find I like your mother's company quite a lot."

The prince seemed to relax just a bit. "Okay, then."

While he'd told Michelle the truth and could stay in Mallard Lake Township for a while, time was something Tony really didn't have the luxury of. "She's all you have?"

"Yes."

"Michelle told me she's your aunt. What happened to your parents?"

"Killed in a car accident when I was little."

"Siblings?" Did he know he had a sister somewhere out there?

Nicholas hesitated for just a second, something most people wouldn't notice but with Tony's knowledge of Nicholas's background, it stood out like a red flag in front of a bull. "No." He took a drink of the water, likely to cover his nervousness over the question.

So he knew about Christiana, but likely not much more than that. "When were your parents killed?"

"When I was very young. Michelle has raised me ever since."

"I'm sorry to hear you've experienced so much loss, but glad you have someone who loves you." Tony mentally sized Nicholas up. "Do you remember your parents at all?"

Nicholas took another drink and shook his head. "Not really. I have a few vague impressions, but that's about it."

"I'm sure you've seen pictures though."

The prince shredded a napkin. "They were all lost in a fire."

Michelle was creative, all right. It suddenly occurred to Tony the accident with Nicholas's phone might not have been an accident after all. Smart. "I'm sorry to hear that," he said again.

"The only real connection I have to my old life from before the accident is a tenuous one at best." Nicholas shrugged. "It's just not something I think about very often."

"What connection is that?" Would he keep talking if Tony pressed a bit more?

"I guess my father and his best friend hoped I'd marry his daughter."

Tony's breath caught in his throat.

"She's out there somewhere, but I've never met her. Mom gets new pictures of her sometimes though and tells me about how I was supposed to marry Eve."

A multitude of emotions swirled inside Tony. Michelle hadn't forgotten or purposely ignored the upcoming wedding. In fact, Tony was now willing to bet she had a plan all along. "Why haven't you met her? If you're supposed to marry her..."

"It was never anything official. It's not like I proposed. Our families were good friends, and they thought it would be cool if I married their daughter." Nicholas's eyes narrowed as he looked straight at Tony. "You ask a lot of questions."

"I have a background in journalism." Or at least in dealing with pushy journalists. Tony had paid attention over the years. "I don't mean to make you uncomfortable. So let's change the subject away from family. What about you? What kinds of things do you like?"

"I like sports. The resorts seem to have a whole bunch of cool stuff to do. I'm hoping to get a job at one of the zip-line places."

"Is that your long term career aspiration?"

"Nah." He fiddled with the straw wrapper some more. "I think I'd like to do something with politics someday or maybe run my own business. My mom told me my biological parents were very powerful people in their business community. I was supposed to inherit everything, but I didn't." He gave Tony a wry grin. "If I had, I wouldn't be looking for a zip line job."

Tony's admiration for Michelle continued to grow. She'd given Nicholas enough to know something of what had happened to his parents, without actually telling the truth. "Were you supposed to marry this other girl to bring two companies together?"

A look of shock spread across Nicholas's face. "You know, I don't know. That might be part of why they wanted me to marry her so badly, Michelle carries her picture in her wallet and made me keep a copy of it in mine. I always had to tell girls who saw it she was a cousin."

Eighth cousins to be exact. "So what happens now if you don't marry her?"

"Not a clue. Life goes on I suppose."

"That it does. What's your next great adventure going to be if you don't get the zip line job?"

"Oh, it doesn't matter if I get the jobs or not. For Christmas last year, I got my mom a cruise. We just got back last week. She got me a trip to Europe. We're going in June right after my birthday."

See? She'd had a plan all along. Tony would bet good money Michelle planned to take him to the palace in Ravenzario, as long as she felt it was safe. If she didn't, she would take him to Mevendia where he would meet his bride.

The bell jangled over the top of the door. Both Tony and Nicholas glanced that way. Nicholas went back to playing with the straw wrapper, but Tony focused on the new man. Something wasn't quite right. He didn't know what it was, but he had a feeling he needed to keep a very close eye on the young man in front of him.

Nicholas went outside while Tony paid the cashier at the front counter. Under the guise of leaving a tip, he returned to the table, making sure no one was watching when he slipped the now-empty water glass into his satchel. He'd send it to Alexander later and get the DNA test done ASAP.

"Why don't we do what now?" Michelle cocked an eyebrow at the man standing in her doorway.

"Why don't we take your son with us?" Anthony asked her.

"Because I don't generally take my son on dates." She crossed her arms. "It's not like he's five, and you'd be raising him if things worked out with us. He's a grown man."

"I know, but I'd like to get to know both of you better." He tried to give her his best smile. "Please? It'll be fun."

She continued to be skeptical. "I don't know, Anthony. A date with my adult son tagging along?"

"Say what now?" A new voice entered the conversation.

He'd gotten that from her. A prince would never talk like that. Michelle turned to see Nicholas coming down the stairs. "Anthony wants to take us both to dinner."

Nicholas looked as skeptical as she'd been. "Why? You didn't grill me enough earlier?"

Grill him? Michelle looked between the two men. "Grill him?" she asked Anthony. "What is he talking about?"

Anthony shoved his hands in his pants' pockets and looked like he should be scuffing the toe of his shoe in the dirt. "We ran into each other in the diner. I wanted to get to know him better because I want to get to know you better. We talked about his parents' accident and some girl his parents wished he'd marry someday. That's about it."

She looked back at Nicholas. "Is that right?"

He gave that shrug she'd come to hate during his teen years. It meant Anthony's story was close enough.

"Okay, then. You two have been bonding. Maybe Anthony's

right, and it's time for the three of us to go out. Get to know each other." How Anthony treated the young man he knew wasn't her biological son would tell her everything she needed to know about his character.

"Good." Anthony's face lit up. "I've got reservations for three at my resort in about half an hour. How's that sound?"

Fancy. It sounded fancy. They hadn't been to many fancy dinners since coming to the States. And she wasn't dressed for fancy. Michelle turned on her heel and started for the stairs. "I'm going to change. Nicky, you need to put on a tie and find that suit coat." She glanced back at Anthony as he stood in the doorway. "Make yourself comfortable. We'll be right back."

Fortunately, Brianna had left most of her clothes here and, when she discovered how little Michelle had brought with her, told her to wear whatever she wanted. Michelle pulled a black dress out of the closet.

Perfect.

A quick change of earrings and a fluff of her hair later, and she walked back down the stairs to her dates.

The whistle didn't come from Anthony, though admiration was written all over his face. Nicholas was the one who'd whistled.

"You clean up nice, Mom. When was the last time we dressed up anyway?" He offered her his arm, and she took it. Technically, she was Anthony's date, but once again, she would learn what she needed to from his reaction.

"I think the last time we dressed up was for your high school graduation. If you'd work a little bit harder on your college courses, we'd be close to wearing them again." There was a hint of reprimand in her voice, enough for Nicholas to understand. She had prayed he'd either finish his college education or be close by the time the wedding rolled around. Instead, he had only about half the credits he'd need to graduate, and he'd yet to declare a major or figure out what would be entailed to actually finish the degree.

Nicholas escorted her outside with Anthony trailing them. When they reached the late model rental car, Nicholas opened the front passenger door for her to get in. He climbed in the back, angling himself so he had enough leg room. Anthony just smiled as he turned on the ignition. "Let's get this party started."

The drive to the resort section of the lake front didn't take long and soon a valet opened Michelle's door for her. It made her realize how much she missed being taken care of. Sure, both of the royal children were her responsibility, but little things - like washing her own clothes, or opening her own doors, or shopping for the children - had all been done by someone else.

Hidden inside her tattered wallet was a photograph no one ever saw, especially not Nicholas. It had been taken by the paparazzi, but she'd managed to print a copy off the Internet a few weeks after their escape. She was sitting on a bench at the park. Nicholas sat on her lap, snuggled into her chest as he napped. Christiana sat next to her, a book open as she struggled to read the words that were a bit too advanced for her. She perse-vered and succeeded, though. She always had.

The little blond girl still held the second spot in Michelle's heart. It was possible she'd see the now-pregnant queen when she returned Nicholas for the wedding, but held out little hope of being remembered.

"Michelle?"

She looked up when Anthony said her name. "Yes?"

"They're ready for us." He extended his elbow. "Shall we?"

Sliding her hand into the crook of his arm, Michelle struggled to throw off the cloak of uncertainty that often threatened to envelop her when she started thinking about her other young charge. She couldn't get rid of it completely and both men noticed. Nicholas sent her concerned looks, while Anthony tried every conversation topic under the sun to get more than a few words out of her. As dinner neared an end, Anthony went to use the men's room, leaving her alone with Nicholas.

"What is it, Mom? And don't tell me nothing."

She gave him a sad smile. "Just thinking about your sister."

"She's not dead. You told me so."

"I know, but I spent a lot of time with both of you when you were young. I still miss her."

"Will we ever see her again?" Nicholas tore off a bit of bread and popped it in his mouth. "If this threat ever goes away?"

Michelle nodded. "I believe, someday, we will." The day was coming she'd have to let go of both of the children she'd loved as her own. Until they returned to Ravenzario, Michelle could pretend Queen Christiana would remember her and greet her like a long-lost friend. Once it took place in reality, the dreams would shatter, and she would be left out of Nicholas's inner circle. Because she loved him, she would let it happen. Whether he decided to take the crown back from his sister or not, the time had come for her to leave his orbit. It hurt like the dickens, but she'd do it because it would be the best thing for him.

At least it looked like she just might have Anthony to come back to. The thought was like a salve on her heart.

Anthony.

She could get used to him.

7

Even after a week, Michelle's morose attitude still sat poorly with Tony. She wasn't telling him everything. He knew far more than she realized, but without knowing who he really was, he couldn't expect her to trust him.

Still, he'd spent as much time with one or both of them as he could. He needed Nicholas to trust him. Michelle, too. Depending on how the next few days went, would he simply let her do what she'd planned all along and take Nicholas back to his homeland or would he intervene and take the prince back himself?

She put on a happy face, but sadness lurked in the depths of her eyes. He wanted to find a way to chase that away, to make her happy. And that meant spending time with her. Not just because he liked to keep an eye on the young prince, but because he was increasingly attracted to the woman who'd given up so much of her life to take care of him. And not just because his gut remained unsettled and would be until they got the prince back home.

"Dinner? Tonight?" She seemed hesitant, turning her attention to wiping down the bakery counter. "We've had dinner together every night for the last week and a half."

"Not like this." He leaned his forearms on the counter. "Let me make you both dinner. We've gone out a lot, and I enjoy it, but let's face it. We could all use a night in. Put on some comfortable clothes and toss a movie in the DVD player."

It took her a minute of contemplation, but she nodded. "That sounds great." Her voice took on a warning tone. "But that means sweats and an old t-shirt that may or may not have holes in it."

Tony grinned. "Sounds perfect to me." He didn't have anything that comfortable with him, though. He'd have to run to the store and get a pair of sweats and a t-shirt. He needed to buy food to make dinner anyway.

"But why don't we order pizza?" Michelle interrupted his thoughts. "That way you don't have to cook."

"I love to cook," Tony pointed out. "I rarely get to."

"Why not?" She seemed genuinely curious.

He shrugged. "I live alone and work long hours." Technically, he had an apartment in the city, but he spent most nights in a room next to his office. Once all of this was over, maybe he could begin living a bit more normally. Vet more security team members. Finally start to loosen up the tight grip he'd kept for so long on the security department. Alexander had been keeping him up-to-date, and nearly everyone had been rounded up. A couple of minor underlings had likely fled the country, but they weren't too worried about them.

After a few more minutes of conversation, Tony left and headed down the street to the markets. Before long, he had what he needed. Comfortable clothes and the ingredients for chicken cacciatore. As he walked out of the market, though, he changed his mind and went back in. Ten minutes later, he emerged with the necessities for a much better plan.

Nicholas let him in when he knocked at the house. Tony told him the plan, and the young man heartily agreed. By the time Michelle made it home, Nicholas had run out to get a movie, and they were both dressed comfortably. While Michelle took a quick shower, Tony started dinner.

Or brinner.

She'd mentioned one time that she loved a good breakfast - pancakes, scrambled eggs, bacon, biscuits and gravy - but she rarely got it. Tony decided breakfast-for-dinner would be a great alternative. Nicholas loved the idea.

And when Michelle returned downstairs in a pair of tattered sweats and an old t-shirt, she lit up. "This is perfect." She looked at the different dishes piled on the table. "I didn't mean all at the same meal, but that's okay. It looks great." As they sat down, she eyed Tony. "You went and bought those clothes didn't you?"

Tony grinned at her. "I'm from out of town. The only really 'kick back at home comfortable' clothes I have with me are pajamas." He winked. "And I don't know you well enough, just yet, ma'am."

She laughed and started to dish up the meal. The three of them talked easily as they ate. Tony felt a bit apprehensive about the movie, though he wasn't sure why. Did he want to sit next to Michelle? Yes. To keep an eye on her in case of some external threat? No. Because she made his heart speed up, and he wanted to be close to her.

And that was dangerous.

At least until all of this was resolved, and she knew his true identity.

She answered his dilemma by sitting in the only chair when they moved into the living room. He and Nicholas sat on opposite ends of the couch, but it wasn't uncomfortable. Nicholas surprised both of them with his choice of movie.

Disney's *Aladdin*.

"It was his favorite when he was little," Michelle explained.

Nicholas rolled his eyes. "It was *your* favorite, Mom. I got it because you haven't seen it in a long time."

"Of course," she replied.

Tony could hear the implications in her voice, ones she didn't know he understood. Nicholas had identified with the "street rat" who wanted to be a prince. Or maybe, without realizing it, the princess who longed to walk about unrecognized among the people.

The undercurrents remained, though they laughed their way through the movie. By the end, Michelle was wiping her eyes. "I always cry," she told him. "When they finally let them be together. When they let Jasmine choose whoever her heart wants. It's not always so cut and dried."

Nicholas still didn't know he had no choice. What would he think when he found out?

And would he, and Princess Yvette, get a happily-ever-after?

"No dinner tonight?"

Michelle could see the disappointment Anthony tried to keep out of his voice as he sat in the bakery.

"Nicky's birthday is today," she reminded him. He'd known that. She'd mentioned it and the upcoming trip to Europe several times. She felt the increasing pressure to get this all sorted out and the deadline loomed closer than she'd like.

"Can I take both of you out then?"

She would like to spend an evening with both them. She liked Anthony, and so did Nicholas, but this was special.

Michelle shook her head. "Thank you for offering, but no. Nicky promised to take me out, just the two of us."

Anthony nodded like he understood. He couldn't, of course, but it was sweet of him to think he did.

She expected him to ask her out for another time, but he didn't. Maybe he would later. He seemed deep in thought, but before she could try to sort it out, the bell above the door jangled.

She turned back to her job. As she boxed up the order, she saw Anthony wave and walk out the door.

Michelle didn't have time to think much about it. The bakery stayed steady the rest of the afternoon. She left at four and took a quick shower before getting dressed up. Anthony had taken both of them to the resort a couple weeks earlier, but this time, Nicky was taking her to a restaurant at a nearby town.

Or so she'd thought.

Nicholas pulled their car into Anthony's resort a couple hours later. "I thought we were going somewhere else?"

"We were going to, but..." He shrugged. "I can't explain it, but it didn't feel...*right*."

The hair on the back of Michelle's neck stood on end. He'd said things like that a few times before and each time they'd moved on quickly because of something she'd noticed.

Was something else about to come at them? Couldn't it wait until they got to Europe? Specifically, one of the Commonwealth countries. Then she'd have help if something happened. She had phone numbers she could call. Emergency phones that had never rung, but waited at the ready.

Just in case.

She did her best to put it out of her mind and focus on dinner with her son. He wanted to talk about the future, about after they got back from their trip. Should he apply for a college locally? What about online? Then it wouldn't matter where they moved. She didn't mention that might make it easier for him to be traced. Michelle had always done her best to cut all ties with their old life when they moved.

Nicholas looked around her as they splurged on dessert. He waved someone over. Michelle glanced back to see Anthony walking their way, a surprised look on his face.

"What are you two doing here?" he asked. "I didn't think this is where you were going."

She didn't say anything, but let Nicholas answer. To his credit, he didn't say anything about the uneasy feeling. They both liked Anthony, but how well did they really know him?

Anthony gave a slight bow. "I will let you two enjoy your dessert." He clapped Nicholas on the shoulder. "Maybe I can buy you a beer tomorrow." He winked at Michelle. "You're 21 now, right?"

Nicholas grinned. "I am, but I think I'll pass. Thanks. Maybe another time."

He wouldn't want to leave her side until they figured out what made him uneasy. It would be stifling, but it was nice to know he would take care of her so well.

The waiter reappeared with their dessert and the black folder containing their check. Before he could set it down on the table, Anthony took it from him. He wrote on the ticket and seemed to scribble a signature. "My treat," he explained, handing it back to the waiter. "Happy birthday, Nicholas."

Something in the way he pronounced it gave Michelle pause. Nicholas and Nicklaus were often pronounced exactly the same, but technically, they were a tiny bit different. Did Anthony say "Nicklaus" or not? If so, why? A slip of the tongue? Something more?

"Mom?" Nicholas snapped her out of the sudden fear.

"I'm fine." She smiled at both of them, picking up her fork. "This dessert looks great."

After a couple of more words, Anthony left. If only her sense of apprehension would leave so easily.

The next morning, Anthony picked them up for church. Through it all, something still seemed to be bothering Nicholas, but when she asked about it all he said was that he had a lot on his mind. Anthony also seemed preoccupied as they drove to one of the churches in town.

She tried to brush it off, but they both remained that way even after church. It was Anthony's idea to get lunch at a restaurant two towns away. Michelle wasn't sure she wanted to go that far, but when Nicholas agreed, she went along with their plan.

No matter what she tried or how many times she asked, she couldn't get anything out of them. That was going to have to change.

And soon.

8

After a conversation the day before, Tony and Nicholas headed to Mallard Lake Zip Lines while Michelle worked at the bakery again. Just the two of them for a couple of hours would help him get to know the young prince better.

The zip line tour didn't allow a lot of time to talk, though Tony was fairly certain Nicholas would be offered a job soon. One of the management team had been their guide and seemed impressed with Nicholas.

"How about a bite to eat?" Tony asked as they walked back to his car. "My treat."

"Sure." Nicholas grinned while Tony unlocked the car. "I never turn down free food."

They decided on the diner and soon sat in the same booth as before. This time Nicholas took his turn to ask questions.

"Where are you from, Anthony?"

Tony didn't want to lie to the prince, but he certainly wasn't ready to tell the truth either. "A small country in Europe most

Americans have never heard of." At least until Alexander married Queen Christiana and the truth about his identity came out.

Nicholas grinned. "Try me. Mom made sure I knew my European geography. She lived there for a while before my parents died."

Of course she did. "Are you familiar with the Royal Commonwealth of Belles Montagnes?"

Nicholas had to think for a minute. "There are three countries in the Commonwealth, right?"

Tony only nodded.

"I forget their names, but a couple of the royal families have had weddings in the last couple years and some of them married Americans." He shrugged. "That's the only reason I know that much. I did catch Mom watching the ceremonies though. She cried during the last one."

Queen Christiana's wedding?

"It was held in a barn," Nicholas went on. "What kind of royalty has a wedding in a barn? She turned it off when she realized I was in the room and said it wasn't my kind of television, but I did see that much."

Definitely Queen Christiana's wedding. It made sense that she would watch it and cry but also that she didn't want Nicholas to put anything together. "The wedding was supposed to have been in the chapel on the same property but an issue with the roof popped up a few weeks beforehand, and it wouldn't be available."

"Okay then." Nicholas studied him for a moment. "Were you there?"

"I didn't attend the wedding ceremony, no." He'd been huddled in a security bunker. "I have met several members of all three royal families though."

"That's cool."

The waitress put their lunches in front of them. "Let me know if y'all want dessert." She slid the check upside down on the table.

"My mom works at Millie's," Nicholas told her. "I'm sure your desserts are wonderful, but she might tan my hide."

The waitress grinned. "They do have the best cupcakes, don't they?" After another minute of conversation, she went back to work.

"Tan your hide?" Tony asked carefully. "Did Michelle really tan your hide?" He couldn't believe she would have. Nothing was inherently wrong in a spanking necessarily, but it still didn't quite fit.

"Nah. She threatened to a few times, but never actually did." He took a big bite of his sandwich, unaware of Tony's conflicting emotions.

The bell above the door jangled and the same man from last time walked in. Tony instantly felt on guard. He needed to get a picture and send it either to Karl or to the staff in Ravenzario to help him figure out if this guy was a threat.

They ate the rest of their lunch in silence. "You ready to go?" he asked Nicholas when he seemed to be finished.

"Yeah. Let's get out of here." The prince shifted in his seat.

"What's wrong?" Tony needed to know if Nicholas sensed something off.

"You know that feeling when you're sure someone is watching you, but you can't figure out who it is or why they would be?"

Tony nodded. He knew that feeling all too well.

"I've been feeling that way off and on since not long after we got here."

"Okay." They wouldn't go to the sheriff, though Tony probably needed to let the man know he was in town as a professional courtesy. "Let's get out of here."

Once they were on the sidewalk and a couple store fronts down, Nicholas seemed to relax. "It's gone, whatever that feeling is. It left as soon as we left the diner."

So Tony's instincts were right. Nicholas hadn't felt it until the man entered, and it disappeared once they were out of sight. He made a snap decision. "Come on, we're going to the police department. We won't come out and accuse anyone of anything, or file a report, but just mention that it seems like there's a stalker around. It may not be just you the guy is targeting." And he'd talk to the man without Nicholas around and tell him a bit more.

Nicholas didn't protest as they turned toward the station. "But we don't really know that he, whoever he is, is targeting me. It could just be a figment of my imagination."

Tony stopped and looked at him. "Listen to me very carefully, Nicholas. When the hair on your arms or the back of your neck stand up?"

Nicholas nodded.

"That's for a reason. It's a God-given radar that tells you something isn't quite right. You may never know what that something was, but you're absolutely right to try to get away from it." He held open the door to the police station. "After you."

Nicholas was still keeping something from her, and Michelle didn't like that one bit.

He and Anthony had met her when she got off work right before dinner. They went to the diner to eat, then Anthony walked them both home.

When they reached the living room, she let loose. "All right. One of you two better tell me what's going on."

Anthony glanced toward Nicholas, but she turned the full force of her glare on Anthony.

Finally, Nicholas answered. "A couple of times this week, I felt like someone was watching me."

Her stomach filled with dread. "What?"

"Someone was watching me."

"Who?"

Anthony answered. "We couldn't figure it out. It could be a nosy busybody trying to sort out the new guy in town or a girl looking for her next boyfriend. We don't know."

Or it could be so much more than that. "It's time for you to go, Anthony." She looked back at Nicholas, regretting what she was going to have to do.

She didn't say the words, but he knew anyway. "No," he told her.

"No what?" Anthony asked, glancing between her and the road.

"No, I'm not moving *again* so soon," Nicholas answered him. "I know what that look means, Mom."

"Move again so soon?" Anthony asked.

"Yeah." Nicholas kept talking even though Michelle gave him her best glare. "My parents didn't just die in an accident. They were killed. My dad was a powerful man, and someone would do anything to stop him. Anytime Mom felt someone was getting too close to us, we'd move. And if she didn't feel that way, we'd sometimes move anyway."

"Is that true?" Anthony asked.

Michelle nodded.

"Then you've got the right guy on your side. I know some people who work in security for VIPs. I'll give one of them a call, and he'll get some of his guys up here to help keep an eye on things." He looked directly at her. "Sometimes it's better to stay and deal with the threat than leave and never know when it's going to find you."

Was he *actually* questioning her and how she took care of Nicholas growing up? Michelle tried to contain her anger, but it seeped through every pore. Her nails dug into the palms of her hands as her fists clenched tighter.

"I'm not saying you should have stayed and faced it ten or fifteen years ago," he went on. "I'm not even saying you should have stayed and faced it this last time. I'm saying you have me now and, if in fact there is someone sinister watching Nicholas, I know how to deal with threats like this. Let me help you."

The idea of letting someone else take charge of the worrying held great appeal for Michelle. Finally, she nodded. "Fine."

"Good. Let's get your things. You're going to stay at the resort with me."

With him? "I don't think so, Anthony." She would take care of Nicholas's safety. Just like she always had.

"I'll call and get a suite," Anthony told her. "I'm not suggesting anything improper, but it will be best for you two to stay close to each other if something were to happen."

He probably had a point. It didn't take long for them to pack their suitcases and put them in the trunk of Anthony's rental car. As she went to climb into the passenger seat, though, the hair on the back of her neck stood on end. Michelle looked around, but didn't see anything out of the ordinary.

"You feel it, too, don't you, Mom?" Nicholas rested a hand on her back. "Let's get out of here."

Michelle climbed in and pulled her seatbelt on. "I think that's a great idea, Nicky." She kept an eye out as they drove, noting that Anthony didn't take a direct route, but turned down several side streets at random intervals.

"No one's following us?" she asked.

"Not that I can tell." Anthony took two more quick turns in rapid succession. "If there was, I think we've lost them. Regardless, I'm not going back to the main street to get out of town. That would be the easiest way for someone to pick us back up." He turned again onto a wooded street and stopped on one side. They stayed there for a couple of minutes while he looked something up in the map app on his phone. After he found what he was looking for, they started moving again.

Taking the back roads to the resort took far longer than the direct route, but Anthony used the time to call and ask for a suite.

Now that she'd felt someone watching them, Michelle couldn't shake the feeling. Staying in the same area, even in a safer location, went against the grain. They should be on the move, going far away. Her fight or flight instinct definitely tended toward flight.

But at the same time, she could envision the worst case scenarios. Spending the last nearly two decades looking over her shoulder, she'd thought of every possible outcome. This time it likely included this unknown person following them as they left town and somehow getting them to stop on a deserted road and then never being seen again.

Maybe it was time to stand up. To say enough is enough and meet the threat head on. If this person could find them all the way in tiny Mallard Lake Township, Minnesota, he could find them anywhere.

Trust didn't come easy for her, and it surprised her to realize she trusted Anthony after only knowing him a couple of weeks. She prayed her trust in him was well-founded.

fter a quick stop at the front desk and another in his old room to gather his things, Tony opened the door to a suite on the top floor of the resort. "There's one bed in that room," he told Michelle. "Why don't you take it? Nicholas and I will share the other room." In reality, he'd sleep in the living area, if he slept at all.

What he needed to do was find a safe house in the area. A place they could bolt if they needed to, somewhere that wouldn't be connected to any of them. Karl would be in town by early afternoon and coordinate with the local police. He would help find a place, though they wouldn't be seen together. He'd give as much information to the authorities as strictly necessary and no more. Until then it was up to Tony alone to keep the prince and his nanny safe.

Michelle left her suitcase in the living area while she went to the restroom. When she exited, Tony brought it into her room and set it up on the luggage rack. It didn't sound like clothes, though. It sounded like things hitting against each other.

"What do you have in here?" he asked, not because he *needed* to know, but because he was curious what her answer would be and what kind of things she found to be the most important.

"We left our last place in a hurry and didn't have time to actually move," she explained. "I brought pictures." She unzipped the suitcase. The first thing she brought out was a silver evening gown.

"Awfully fancy for Mallard Lake," he observed.

"It's a beautiful, expensive dress. I have an occasion in mind to wear it and couldn't bear to leave it behind."

The wedding? What else could it be? She hung it up then began removing a few of the picture frames. "Pictures of me and Nicholas as he grew up. That's all. But they mean the world to me."

He could imagine, and he loved seeing bits of the prince's life in exile. But that wasn't what made him stop. "Who's that?" he asked, pointing to one of the pictures.

Michelle picked up the photo and smiled at it, though it seemed a bit wistful. "Eve. The girl Nicky's parents hoped he'd marry."

Eve. Yvette. Close but different enough to make it hard for Nicholas to track her down. He wanted to ask more, but didn't. Nicholas knew he was from the Commonwealth of Belles Montagnes. If Michelle found out, she would know he knew who she was.

His phone rang before anything else could be said. He checked it. Karl. He caught a glimpse of a velvet box in the bottom of the suitcase as he motioned to Michelle that he'd be right back and went out into the living area. Did she have jewels? Her own or the crown's? "What have you got?"

"I got here a couple hours earlier than expected and already spoke with the chief of police. I'm texting directions to an unoccupied cabin and a small cave few people know about." Karl hesitated. "The cave is probably not big enough for the three of you, though."

"Thanks." Tony would look it up on the map app on his phone and come up with the best ways to get there, including by foot if needed. If it came down to it, Nicholas would be the one in the cave. He and Michelle would see to it.

"I'll call if I hear anything. You do the same."

Tony agreed and went back through the open door to Michelle's room.

Her back was to him with her head bowed as she stared out the window overlooking Mallard Lake.

"Are you all right?" he asked moving to her side.

She shook her head. "How can I be all right? All I've done for the last two decades is try to make sure he stays safe."

Tony laid his hand on the small of her back. "You've done an excellent job keeping your charge safe. I'm glad I'm here now to help you."

"I wish it would all just go away. Leave us in peace." She swiped at the tears on her cheeks.

Tony couldn't let her bear it alone any longer. "Come here," he told her softly. "Let me help."

She turned toward him and buried her face in his shoulder. Tony wrapped his arms around her, letting her cry. She didn't stay there long, though. Squaring her shoulders, she pushed away.

"I'm fine," she told him. "A moment of being overwhelmed. That's all."

He didn't let her leave the circle of his arms. "It's okay to let someone else help, Michelle." With one arm he held her close and with the other hand, he brushed the hair off her face. "Let me help you."

"It's my job, Anthony." Her blue eyes stared into his. "Mine alone."

"'Bear ye one another's burdens and so fulfill the law of Christ.' Galatians 6:2. Let me help bear your burden."

"Why would you want to help me?" Her voice was small. "No one has wanted to help me in years."

That wasn't strictly true, and he suspected Michelle knew that. He'd wanted to help her this whole time, but until recently, the best way to do so was to keep his distance. To pretend the prince and his nanny had been swept away by that river to a watery grave.

But he couldn't tell her that. Instead, he told her a different truth. "I'm in awe of how hard you must have worked to keep Nicholas safe. How much of your own life has been put on hold to protect him from whoever would like to see him dead. Your strength amazes me."

"I'm not strong, Anthony. I want to be, but I'm not. I never have been. I've only managed to do what I had to, what was necessary for both of us to survive."

"Very few people could have done everything you've done while maintaining a much needed sense of normalcy for your young charge." His fingers brushed her hair back again. "You are incredible."

No. What he found himself wanting to do was incredible. He wanted to kiss her. To tell her everything. The way her eyes seemed to be searching his, he suspected she wanted the same thing.

For once in his life, Tony decided to throw caution to the wind. He threaded his fingers into Michelle's hair and rubbed his thumb along her cheek. There could be no mistaking what he wanted to do.

Her eyes fluttered closed as he leaned closer. With the first brush of his lips against hers, he was transported to a different time and place. To a day when he and Michaela could be together without any pretense between them.

She kissed him back as fully as he kissed her.

"Mom! Anthony!" The panicked voice in the distance brought him back to the present.

Tony turned, his hand going to his pocket where his concealed weapon resided. "What is it?"

Nicholas's eyes were wide. Tony knew he'd seen the kiss, but he also knew that wasn't what scared the prince.

Nicholas, his eyes wide, looked between Tony and Michelle. "He's here."

What just happened? Michelle tried to shake herself out of her stupor. First, Anthony kissed her and then...what did Nicholas say?

Anthony had moved away with one hand shoved in his pocket. Odd.

"Where?" he asked Nicholas.

"I looked to see what the view was like in the other room, and I saw him down by the pool."

"Are you sure?" Michelle asked him. "We're up fairly high. And who do you think it is?"

Nicholas crossed his arms. "Yes, I'm sure. He was wearing the same bright blue shirt when he came into the diner the other day. That's when I started to feel like I was being watched again."

"Again?" She and Anthony spoke in unison.

"I felt it briefly a couple weeks ago, then nothing so I didn't say anything. I used the lens on my camera to zoom in. It's still a bit blurry but it's him."

Nicholas had a nice camera. She'd made sure he got one when he showed an interest in photography. He gave the camera to Anthony, who looked at the pictures.

"It's him," Anthony concurred, pulling out his phone. "I've been told about a local safe house, but we need to get out without him realizing we're gone." She could almost see the gears turning in his head. "That means my car is out. It needs to stay here. So do the suitcases. I'll have my contact keep an eye on the room."

"What about a hike?" Nicholas tossed out the idea. "Make a big deal about just going for a couple hours, take a couple bottles of water with us, and take off. Meet someone not too far from here."

Anthony nodded slowly. "It has merit, but I'm afraid he'll come after you two if he knows we're out in the woods unprotected. It would be better if he doesn't know we're leaving at all."

"What about a delivery vehicle?" Michelle put that out for consideration.

Anthony thought that over. "That's a good idea. We can go down a service elevator and have Karl pick us up in a windowless van and take us to the safe house." He pulled his phone out and sent a text. Within a few seconds, there a reply came through. "He'll be here in about thirty minutes unless we hear something else from him."

"Who is this guy?" Nicholas asked her. "What does he want with me, anyway?"

Soon she would have to tell him everything, but not yet. "I don't know, Nicky." The truth. Not entirely the whole truth but close enough. She hated how much she was justifying her statements in the last few days. She turned to Anthony. "Do we wait here or do we go downstairs and find somewhere to hide while we know where he is?"

Anthony pulled up a floor plan for the hotel on his phone. He zoomed in and out a few different times then tapped around some more. "If we go down the service elevator, there's a conference room that appears to be vacant at the moment. At least, there's nothing listed in there on today's schedule of events. We can slip in there until Karl gets here."

It seemed as good a plan as any Michelle would be able to come up with. She looked back through the window to the lounge area around the pool. "He's still there."

"Then let's go." Anthony's mouth was set in a grim line. She had to look away or it would be too easy to remember the intensity with which he had kissed her just a few moments earlier.

The service elevators weren't far, but Anthony made her and

Nicholas wait in an alcove not visible from the main hallway. Surely this man couldn't make it upstairs that quickly. The elevator arrived, and Anthony glanced down the hallway one more time. "Let's go," he ordered quietly.

Once inside, he motioned them to the side where they would be the most hidden should something happen when the door opened. As they descended, Anthony turned to them. "If I tell you to do something, do it. Don't ask questions, just act. Promise me."

Michelle glanced at Nicholas. He didn't seem unduly upset by the instruction, but she wasn't sure. She didn't question him out loud, but a thought struck her. They had known this man less than a month, and somehow he'd taken charge of protecting her young prince.

Could she be guilty of letting a handsome man turn her head? Convince her to take him into her confidence then prove to be unworthy of that trust?

As the elevator doors opened, Anthony checked outside. "It's clear." When they reached the swinging "employees only" entrance to the service area, he motioned to them. "Stay behind me."

He opened the door just enough to see out one direction then opened the other door just enough to peek out that way. When he was satisfied the coast was clear, he opened the door further.

"Let's go," Anthony told them quietly.

With her heart in her throat, they hurried down the hall and around the corner. The door to the conference room didn't open easily, but Anthony managed to get it unlocked and let them precede him in while he kept an eye out for danger.

"So now what?" Nicholas asked.

"We wait. Stay out of view of the window in the door. He shouldn't have any reason to look for us here." Anthony kept his phone out, checking it repeatedly until the tensest twenty minutes Michelle had experienced in many years passed.

Anthony stuck his phone back in his pocket. "Okay. It's time."

He went to the door and peeked out. "Stay behind me and stay close."

Nicholas motioned for her to go first, something that puzzled Michelle. He'd always been so protective of her. Then she realized he was looking for danger coming from the rear. He'd taken the role that had been hers, should still be hers. *He* was the Crown Prince, the rightful ruler of Ravenzario. *He* was the one who needed protecting.

They made it to a side door. Anthony checked his phone once more before motioning them closer. "The van's right outside the door." Another text came in. "Let's go."

He opened the door and waited for Michelle and Nicholas to pass him and enter the open back doors of the van. In just a few seconds, he pulled the doors shut behind them.

None of them spoke to the driver, which Michelle thought was odd, but the van drove off. The drive seemed to take forever though it likely didn't last nearly as long as it seemed. Turns and curves, hills and valleys, smooth and finally rough roads led to this so-called safe house. She expected to be a bundle of nerves, but the prayers seemed to be working. She'd prayed for many years that God would send the help they needed when they needed it. He had, over and over. Whether it was new friends in Boaz or a house selling quickly or a nurse who knew what to do about bee stings, God had provided for them repeatedly. Tony, with his connections, seemed to be another one of those provisions.

The driver didn't get out when the van stopped. Anthony spoke quietly with him for a moment then opened the side door. "We're here. It's safe."

Michelle and Nicholas both looked around cautiously, though all she saw was woods until her eyes landed on the cabin. If that was "just" a cabin, the Ravenzarian royal palace was "just" a house.

"Come on." Anthony hurried them into the now-opened garage. "Get inside."

A minute later, they all sat in the living room. Anthony looked her straight in the eyes. "It's time."

"What?" Time for her to do what exactly?

He continued to look straight at her. "It's time, Michaela."

Her heart stopped.

"Time to tell Nicklaus who he really is."

10

Tony could see the emotions cross Michaela's face. Surprise followed rapidly by fear and then a fierce protectiveness.

"How do you know that?"

"Know what?" Nicklaus interjected. "Mom, why did he call you Michaela?"

She kept her eyes on Tony's. "Because it is my given name, just as yours is not Nicholas but Nicklaus David Richard Antonio, Crown Prince of Ravenzario."

Tony tried to convey his sympathy through his eyes. It couldn't be an easy thing for either one of them.

Nicklaus had to clear his throat twice before he could speak. "Say what now?"

Michaela seemed to have trouble getting her emotions under control. Tony answered for her. "Your parents were His Majesty King Richard and Her Majesty Queen Marissa of Ravenzario. Nearly eighteen years ago, on December 23, their car with you and Michaela inside, went over a cliff and landed with the engine submerged in an icy river. The queen died as emergency services made it to her side. The king died not long afterward, before he could be removed from the vehicle. The bodies of Crown Prince Nicklaus and his nanny were never found. They were declared dead and empty caskets were buried at the same time as the king and queen."

"How do you know all this?" Michaela whispered.

"My name is Tony Browning. The day before the accident I was promoted to Head of Security for the Royal Family of Ravenzario. I was the only one King Richard spoke to before his death. He told me to find a particular file folder in one of the archives no one ever looked in. In that folder was the barest of information to allow me to begin a search for you when it was safe."

"It's been almost two decades." She struggled to hold back tears. "Why haven't you come before now?"

"In that paperwork was enough information for me to begin an investigation against Henry Eit, alleged half-brother of Queen Marissa. It wasn't until about two years ago that we finally had what we needed to arrest him. Even then, he'd infiltrated the palace so thoroughly we had to be exceptionally careful who we trusted. Queen Christiana's fiancé was discovered to be one of his minions and planned to kill her on their honeymoon. That's how close Henry came to total control. Her fiancé was arrested two weeks before the wedding, and she married Duke Alexander instead."

"That was nearly a year ago."

"It was. But I am sure you are aware of the much more recent release of Henry Eit from prison, and his subsequent assassination attempt against the queen. During that investigation, we finally found his hidden office, filled with the papers we needed to wrap this up once and for all. The arrests were many and swift. I left Duke Alexander in charge of the continuing investigation while I began the long overdue search for Prince Nicklaus." He gave her a pointed look. "I'm quite certain you understand why I needed to come now."

"Yes." Her voice cracked. "I do."

"Well, I don't!" Nicklaus jumped up. "And it's about time one of you talked to *me*."

Tony stood and bowed slightly at the waist. "You are Crown Prince Nicklaus. You and your sister were both to have died in the car accident. Your sister's bout with the flu saved her life. Michaela saved yours. Since I found the folder two days after the accident, I have prayed daily for your continued safety and for the doors to open when it was time for me to find you. I traced you to the Sovereign Commonwealth of Athmetis. The Lord led me to the right person, and I found Yaya, the woman who hid you in the secret room in her courtyard for nearly a month."

"Then you went to Louisiana, didn't you?" Michaela asked the question. "It was our first stop when we arrived in the States."

"I did," he confirmed. "I met a young lady who saw you both in Florida a few weeks ago."

"Then Norma Jean called me and told me someone was asking questions. We left Edwardsville a few minutes later."

He told them how he traced them to Mallard Lake Township and wondered if this other man hadn't followed him somehow. Or if he could have broken into that house and pulled the same information off the computer Karl and Tony had.

Tony could see Nicklaus trying to absorb it all. "So, if I'm the Crown Prince, why is this sister queen?"

"Because your safety depended on Henry believing you were dead. Very, very few people knew for certain your bodies were never found. Rumors have swirled off and on, but to the best of my knowledge, Henry still believes you died in that river."

"What about my parents?"

Tony turned to see tears falling down Michaela's cheeks again. "I'm sorry, Michaela. We couldn't let them know. We needed the world to believe you were both dead. The queen was only told after the arrest of her uncle, but all she was told was that your bodies had never been found. She still doesn't know your survival was likely."

"Then how are you here?" Michaela demanded. "Why aren't you still protecting Christiana?"

"You know why I'm here," he reminded her quietly. "Duke Alexander urged me to come, but as far as anyone else knows, I'm taking a long overdue vacation."

"If I'm Crown Prince, why is my sister queen?" Nicklaus demanded again. "I get that everyone had to believe I was dead, but what happens now? I pop into Ravenzario and go 'hey sis! I'm not dead! Beat it!'"

Tony shook his head. "It would not be quite so simple, no."

Michaela pulled something out of her wallet. "I've kept this hidden for years, but it's time for you to see it." She handed the picture to Nicklaus. "That's you, me, and your sister not long before the accident."

Tony could see the young man working to put it all together.

"The pictures of my family weren't lost in a fire, were they?"

"No, but if I had shown you photos, and you'd ever seen anything about the Ravenzarian royal family, you would have known, and I couldn't risk you letting it slip."

Tony spoke gently to Nicklaus. "In the last twenty years, Michaela has done nothing but sacrifice everything to protect you. She hasn't seen her family or her friends since before the accident. She allowed all of them to believe she was dead so she could keep your survival a secret. She loves you as a mother loves her son and don't ever doubt that."

Nicklaus went to stare out a window overlooking the lake, no doubt trying to assimilate everything thrown at him in the last half hour.

"Are my parents still alive? I know they were a year ago, but still?" Michaela drew his attention back to her. "My brothers and sister?"

Tony turned back to her, his heart heavy. "Your parents are very much alive, though your mother has had multiple heart attacks. She's doing well last I heard. So is your younger brother. He's married with a son. In fact, your father walked the queen down the aisle at her wedding. Your brothers' children were the ring bearer and flower girl. Your sister and sister-in-law stood up with the queen. Your brother stood with the duke."

Tears colored her voice. "I saw, but there was nothing about my other brother."

"Your other brother..." Tony sighed. "Your brother, Dustin, his wife, and one of their children were killed when a bridge collapsed during a Medicane a couple of years ago. The maintenance had been defunded by Henry over the years. The flower girl at the wedding is their daughter, being raised by Joseph."

Her shoulders heaved, and Tony pulled her into his arms.

"I'm so sorry," he whispered. "You've sacrificed everything for Ravenzario, and this is how you're repaid. Your brother and his family were also victims of Henry Eit."

Her tears continued, becoming full body-wracking sobs, as she absorbed all that she'd lost.

In that moment, Tony would have given almost anything to take away her pain. If only she would let him.

Michaela had always known telling Nicklaus the truth wouldn't be easy. She'd never expected to have help. She'd rarely let herself think about her parents, or her siblings, whether they knew she was alive or what became of them. The few glimpses at the wedding had been like water in the driest desert.

But here, with Tony's arms around her, she almost felt safe. She didn't feel alone for the first time in many years. Prince Nicklaus had always been with her, but it wasn't a relationship of shared burdens. She had never been able to tell him enough about his history, about the danger, for him to shoulder part of the load with her.

"Is this why we were going to Europe for my birthday?" Nicklaus didn't turn from the window.

A hiccup shook her body.

Tony answered for her. "Yes. Your twenty-first birthday is significant, and I knew as soon as you told me about the trip, this was why. To take you home."

To take him home. Leave her prince in Europe with his family and his bride. Return to her life in the United States, but the reality hit her. For the last few weeks, she'd hoped Anthony would be waiting for her when she came back. *Tony* would be back at work in the Ravenzarian palace, not helping clean tables in Millie's Bakery.

Tony hadn't mentioned the wedding yet. Why not? Afraid Nicklaus would refuse to go? Princess Yvette had grown into a lovely young woman and all reports seemed to indicate that she was kind as well. Would Nicklaus refuse to marry her? Is that what concerned Tony?

"Sir?" Tony still had his arms around her, but he spoke to Nicklaus.

Nicklaus turned around. "Me?"

"Yes, sir. Would you please move away from the windows? We all need to find a less visible location to continue this conversation."

"I'm not a 'sir,'" Nicklaus grumbled. "Never have been."

"On the contrary." Tony turned, leaving one arm around her shoulders. "You were born into one of the oldest ruling families in the world. Your birth was celebrated by at least three countries. You are His Royal Highness, Crown Prince Nicklaus David Richard Antonio of Ravenzario. You have several other titles that go along with it. You are a duke twice over, a count, and an honorary member of the Ravenzarian military. You would have commanded men if you had stayed in Ravenzario and not been required to take the throne until after your time of military service ended. You are the very definition of a man people address as 'sir.' A DNA test has already been done proving you are a full sibling to the queen."

Nicklaus glared at him.

Michaela hiccupped again. "When did you do that?"

"The prince came to talk to me at the diner. He drank a glass of water. I sent the glass back to Ravenzario to have it tested. Now, sir, would you please move away from the window and join us in the master suite? I'm told there is a sitting area in there and the windows are curtained. For your own safety, we need to move."

He still glared, but this time he moved away from the window and toward the double doors on the far end of the room. Michaela pulled herself away from the comforting embrace and followed him into the lavishly appointed bedroom and sitting area. Nicklaus flopped quite unceremoniously onto the couch.

She sat across from him. "Nicky..."

His glare cut off her words. "You've lied to me my whole life."

She opened her mouth to respond, but he held up a hand.

"Sorry, not my whole life, just since we moved to the States." His sarcasm was biting.

"Nicky," she tried again. "If you hate me, if you never want to see me again once this is all over, I understand." It would rip her heart out, but she would let him go. "Just know that *everything* I've done since the day you were born was to protect you. First, from scrapes and falls, and then to protect your very life since we escaped from that car." Another painful hiccup interrupted her speech. "And I love you more than you can imagine."

He looked over at her, the hard lines on his face gradually softening. "I know, Mama. Just give me some time." He sat up and swung his legs over until his feet rested on the floor. "I've always known you weren't my biological mother, but finally knowing more about who they were makes calling you that a bit more odd."

Michaela gave him her very best smile. "I have been honored to be your mother all these years, but you're right. It's time to put that part of our lives to the side and to protect you from this threat. Once this is over and you return to Ravenzario, it will be time for you to get on with your life as a prince. I am not your mother. I never was. I will see you safely home to your family and pray for your continued good health and well-being."

He jumped up and came to her side in two large steps. Nicklaus knelt in front of her. "Mama, you may not be my biological mother. I've always believed my parents must have loved me very much if they left me in your care, because I couldn't have asked for anyone better. Will I continue to call you 'Mom' when we go to Europe? It seems like that would be a bad idea, but why don't we cross that bridge when we get to it? Isn't that what you always told me?"

Michaela reached out and cradled his face in her hand. "My sweet boy..."

Before she could finish the statement she hadn't fully formed in her mind, Tony interrupted them. "We won't be here long."

She and Nicklaus turned in unison to look at him.

"I know you two would like to talk, but right now, the primary goal is to keep Prince Nicklaus alive. Preferably all three of us, of course, but our primary directive is to protect the prince."

He looked straight into Michaela's eyes, and she knew he understood. She would have always given her very life to protect this young man, but for the first time in a long time, it seemed plausible that she would be asked to.

Michaela gave him a slight nod, and Tony returned it. She placed both hands on either side of Nicklaus's face and pressed a kiss against his forehead. He wouldn't realize it, but she was saying good-bye. Before all of this ended, she would either have given her life in protection of her prince, or he would move on into his new life. Either way, she treasured these last moments before everything went haywire. She rested her forehead on his as her heart whispered a prayer.

She released him and turned to Tony. "What do we need to do?"

11

This situation was going to be tough on both of the people in the room. He knew Michaela fully expected to be cut out of Nicklaus's life before long. That would be difficult on any mother, biological or not.

And Nicklaus would be taken from the only life he'd ever known, thrown into a wedding to a woman he'd never met and into a royal life Michaela had tried to prepare him for but couldn't, not without the resources of the palace and telling him the whole truth. He was a polite, generous young man, and those qualities would serve him well when he returned to palace life.

But first they had to get him out of the country. The Bayfield family plane was on its way from Ravenzario. It had been decided the royal plane would cause too much suspicion. Even if it had been stateside already, until they knew who this man was, where he was from and for certain they were safe, it was too much of a risk.

Michaela repeated her question before he finally answered it. "I have a feeling we're all going to need our rest. Why don't you both lie down for a while?"

Nicklaus stood. "Take the bed, Mama. I want to speak with Tony for a few minutes."

Michaela stared at them both then went into the attached bathroom, likely to splash some water on her face.

When they were alone, Nicklaus turned to Tony. "I want to be very clear. I get that I'm some kind of prince, but Michaela? She's to be kept safe, even at my expense."

The directive didn't surprise Tony, but that didn't mean he would follow it. "My first priority, sir, is the protection and safety of the royal family. With that said, I will do everything in my power to keep both of you safe."

Nicklaus crossed his arms over his chest. "Are you falling for her?"

Tony raised an eyebrow. "Pardon?"

"I saw you kissing her. Are you falling for her?"

"That's irrelevant." His heart *had* become involved, despite his best intentions. It pained him to say, but if he had to choose between the two of them, he would choose Nicklaus. It was his sworn duty.

Nicklaus started to say something else, but the bathroom door opened, and Michaela reentered the room. She looked between the two of them, but didn't say anything.

"I think we're safe for the time being," Tony told both of them. "It's not until after dark that I would expect anything to happen."

"It will be dusk soon," Nicklaus pointed out. "Are we planning to move after dark?"

Tony shook his head. "Not unless we need to." His phone buzzed, and he pulled it out of his pocket. "I need to take this. Both of you get some rest."

He answered the phone, speaking Italian to Prince Alexander on the other end. It seemed likely that Michaela had some knowledge of the language, but he didn't expect Nicklaus would. He would need to take language classes when things settled down.

Tony gave the prince consort an update and received one in

return. Queen Christiana was taking it easy but doing well. Alexander was still healing from being shot during the assassination attempt, but was also doing well. The arrests were nearly complete, and a number of people had decided it was better to cooperate than continue to fight the inevitable.

It was in one of those interrogations that they had discovered this man who now stalked them. He had been one of Henry's most trusted lieutenants, but also completely off their radar. He had military experience and should be considered very dangerous.

Tony disconnected the call and returned to the bedroom, relieved to find the lights out and both Michaela and Nicklaus resting, though he didn't know how comfortable Nicklaus's couch was. They would hole up here for the night and, as long as everything remained quiet, they would leave in the morning. Karl would come get them and the Bayfield plane would be waiting by then.

Distant thunder caught his ear. Not the best background for a night when he needed to be sharp and hear even the slightest sounds. A quick check of the weather app on his phone told him thunderstorms were likely off and on all night. He would need to be extra vigilant.

Hours passed with Tony doing everything he knew to do to stay alert. He played mental games with himself and did exercises, among other things. One storm rolled through, followed by a period of calm and then another storm.

It wasn't until the fourth storm rolled through that Tony's hair stood on end. Something didn't sound quite right. Rather than waiting to figure out what it was, he shook Nicklaus awake, putting his hand over the prince's mouth until recognition kicked in.

"Is someone here?" Nicklaus whispered.

"I'm not sure, but I don't want to wait. Get your coat on."

Nicklaus nodded and did as Tony asked while he went to wake Michaela. Her eyes were wide with fear as he also covered her mouth to keep her from crying out. In just a few minutes, they were ready to leave if they needed to.

Thunder struck again, but this time, the sound of wood splintering could also be heard.

The front door had been breached.

"This way," Tony breathed. He led them through the bathroom, into the closet, and opened the door to one of several wardrobes found inside. Why did they have wardrobes inside a closet? Tony had no idea. The wardrobe, like the one in Professor Digory Kirke's house that led to Narnia, was so much more than it looked. Inside, were fur coats and underneath them, somewhat obscured, was a narrow, circular staircase. Without being told, Michaela and Nicklaus started down. As Tony pulled the door shut behind him, the beam of a flashlight could be seen in the outer room. He prayed this staircase was as secret as he'd been told. Moving as silently as possible, he descended. At the bottom, he found Nicklaus and Michaela a few steps down the corridor.

"Keep going," he whispered. "Stop at the door."

If his information was correct, the door was well-hidden just beyond the tree line. If they could get there and into the woods, they would be safe.

Visions of another night spent hiding in the woods threatened to overwhelm Michaela as they hurried through the trees. This time she didn't carry a toddler destined to be king, but in many ways, it was more terrifying. If she'd failed then, no one would have blamed her. It would have been the fault of the accident, or the freezing water, or the cold night. Now, it would be because she had called and texted a friend from several moves ago on her cell phone and left access to the records unprotected.

Stupid. Stupid. Stupid.

"Where are we going?" Nicklaus called from behind her, his voice nearly drowned out by the storm. At least this water wasn't only a degree or two above frigid, but that was the only good thing she could say about the storm.

Tony glanced back but didn't answer, a well-timed flash of lightning showed annoyance written all over his face.

When Tony reached the next thick clump of trees, he stopped and waited for them to catch up. "I'm told there's another place to hide up here."

"What makes you think this guy is closing in?" Nicklaus asked. "There's no way he could have found that staircase."

Tony leaned in closer. "I don't know how he left the house, but I've seen a light following us. We can't linger here. We can't slow down. We have to get to another place of safety."

When they started walking again, it seemed to be along a small trail. A game trail maybe? Whatever it was, it was covered with leaves and other forest-y debris so it seemed unlikely they could be leaving footprints. The storm would cover up most of the noises they made as they walked.

After another ten or fifteen minutes, Tony stopped again.

"How much farther?" she whispered.

"Not far, I think," he replied. "But we have a choice to make. Fast or careful? There's a clearing ahead. I think we're far enough ahead of him that if we run across, he won't see us. Going around will keep us under cover, but it's significantly longer."

"Let's run," Nicklaus decided. "I want to get this over with." Another flash of lightning told her his concern was for her, not himself. He wanted her safe.

Tony agreed and admonished them, again, to stay close. They skirted the first part of the clearing, until they reached a large rock. At that point, Tony waited for them to be together, then took her hand. They ran across the open field.

Michaela prayed as she hadn't prayed in many years, and that was saying something. Lightning needed to hold off for another minute or two until they were safely in the cover of the woods again. She breathed a sigh of relief as they reached the trees.

After another few minutes of walking, Tony stopped them. He waited for another flash of lightning to choose their direction. In a few feet, he stopped next to a large rock, pulling aside some greenery hanging against it. Behind it, a small hole opened up.

"Get in," Tony instructed.

Michaela pushed Nicklaus, but he refused to move. Frustrated, she went in first with Nicklaus following her.

"There's not enough room," she whispered to Nicklaus. "I can't go any further."

He wrapped an arm around her shoulders. "I would imagine Tony knew that all along. He's either outside keeping watch or laying a trail for this man to follow away from here."

She had known for many years that those who pledged to protect the crown would, quite literally, lay down their lives to protect the royal family. Despite the strange twists and turns her life had taken, she never expected to see it in action. "Dear God, keep him safe," she whispered.

"Amen," Nicklaus whispered back.

Michaela's prayer didn't end, even as she wrapped her arms around the prince's waist. They stood there, with no way to know the passage of time. Her dripping hair began to dry and her clothes no longer felt quite as heavy, though the denim of her jeans definitely felt stiff.

"Mama?" His quiet voice seemed abnormally loud.

"Hush." She whispered though he hadn't.

He ignored her. "If I'm the Crown Prince, who's Eve?"

She knew the question would come sooner or later. For now, she simply refused to answer.

The minutes stretched on until she was certain the night must have passed. Michaela knew it was her mind playing tricks on her. This storm hadn't ended, but still increased in its intensity.

They both tensed when they heard a shout in the distance.

Nicklaus stepped toward the opening, but Michaela didn't let him go. She knew he wouldn't drag her into the storm, and she used that to her advantage. He needed to stay safe.

More shouting could be heard, this time closer. Nicklaus tensed again, but didn't leave. Not until the shouting became more distinct did he wrench himself away.

The words were close. "Nicklaus! Help!"

Before Michaela could hold him back and remind him that Tony wouldn't call for his help, her not-so-little prince was gone. With that move, she was left no choice. She couldn't stay hidden while the men she loved were in danger.

She recognized the feelings, but refused to dwell on them. Peeking out from the vines, she couldn't see much, but she did remember nearly tripping over a branch not too far away. If it wasn't too heavy, could she wield it as a weapon?

Quietly, she slipped from her hiding spot, lightning illuminating a three-man fight on the other side of the small clearing in front of the rock. Her hair plastered itself to her head as the rain drenched her once again. With a second flash, she found the branch and picked it up, sidling along the trees toward the men.

Two of them she wouldn't hurt for the world, but the other one would discover just how far she would go to protect them. Feeling her way, and using those flashes of lightning judiciously she made her way to the other side. By the time she did, one man was on the ground. Tony? He didn't move.

Michaela wanted to rush to his side, to reassure herself that he lived, but that would have to wait. She saw Nicklaus stumble and the other man pointed something at him. A gun? She was close but not quite close enough or at the right angle to see.

She didn't wait to find out.

Two steps, then, with everything in her, she swung the sturdy branch at the other man's head.

It connected.

The reverberation traveled up the branch and through her

arms. She feared it hadn't been enough, but after the longest second of her life, he fell on top of Nicklaus.

Nicklaus pushed him off and scrambled to his feet, but he wasn't the one she rushed to.

Michaela threw herself to her knees next to Tony, praying he was okay. With adrenaline born of desperation, she rolled him onto his back. As he settled into the wet ground a moan made its way to her ears. She looked at Nicklaus to see he had the weapon and was tying the man's legs up.

Michaela collapsed onto Tony's chest, sobs shaking her. It was finally over.

12

Tony's first thought upon awakening was that someone must have beaten him with a sledgehammer.

His second was that a weight rested on his chest.

The third was that it was still pouring.

He struggled to sit up, displacing whatever it was holding him down. "Nicklaus!"

A light flashed across him. That couldn't be right.

"He's all right," Michaela said. She must have been on his chest, because she knelt next to him.

Tony managed to pull his phone out. Could he call Karl? No bars.

They needed a plan.

"He's out cold," Nicklaus called. "I don't want to try to carry him, but I don't think we want to leave him here either." He held out the gun the man had carried, butt first.

Tony took it from him. "Then what's our plan?"

"We wait?" Nicklaus suggested. "I'm not sure what else to do. Splitting up is out of the question."

Tony stood, his head hanging for a moment as he tried to clear it out and get his bearings. "We're not that far from the lake. From there we may be able to see how far we are from another house."

Michaela turned on her phone's flashlight. "I'll go. You two stay here."

He didn't like that plan but it was the best one they had.

"I've got his feet tied together with my belt," Nicklaus called. "Do you have one for his hands?"

"No." Why hadn't he worn one? "I think, once Michaela gets back, you and I each take one of his arms and drag him along. That will be easier than carrying him, and I can't seem to make myself care about his comfort."

"Me, either."

Tony shined his own flashlight around to see Nicklaus sitting squarely on the man's back. That was one way to keep him down.

"You're falling for Michaela, aren't you?" Nicklaus asked.

Tony couldn't lie to him. "I am."

"Don't hurt her. The more I've found out tonight, the more I've discovered just how amazing she is. I always knew it, but I'm learning the true depth of her love for me. I can't fathom why she would give up everything just to protect me."

"Because she loved you and your family," Tony told him. "She doesn't see it as giving up anything. She sees it as spending her life protecting what was most precious to her in this world."

"How do you know that?"

"Because it's exactly how I feel. Most of my predecessors as head of security for the family have had lives and families of their own. It was more than a job, but it wasn't an obsession. For me, it came dangerously close. Making sure no one discovered you might be alive. Keeping your sister safe. To this day, Henry doesn't realize he sent her to live with the Montevarian royal family because I thought it was the best place for her. I protested mightily when it was suggested, knowing that would make him all the more likely to do it. I've spent my entire working life, since I was fifteen, serving the family. Now that Henry and his minions have been brought down, maybe I can start building a life of my own. That's how I know how she feels."

"And you think she could be part of that family you want to make?"

"I don't know, but I know she's petrified that you'll get one taste of royal life and forget her very existence. Not because she believes you don't love her," he continued over Nicklaus's protests. "But because she knows that life can be overwhelming, and you'll need all kinds of things she won't be able to give you anymore. I'm certain she believes she'll go from being your mother in almost every way to relegated to sitting with the ancillary members of the household staff at important functions. If she's invited at all."

Nicklaus turned that over in his mind. "For my whole life, she's been my mother. Returning to Ravenzario won't change that."

"I know you believe that, and it may not, but there's a very real possibility, that even unintentionally, she will be cut out of your life."

The young prince shook his head. "I won't let that happen. If I'm the rightful king, you work for me, right?"

Tony nodded. "I suppose you could look at it that way, but my primary responsibility is protecting the family not following orders when those two things contradict."

"Fine. But as Prince Nicklaus, I can give you an instruction, and as long as it doesn't interfere with protecting the family, you have to follow it?"

"It's not quite so cut and dried, but yes. If you told me to go wax the floor in the ballroom, I'd likely have your head examined, but within reason, I'll follow instructions." How odd to think that just a few hours after learning his heritage, Prince Nicklaus was already willing to throw some of his weight around.

"Take care of my mother, Anthony. Whether you end up romantically linked or not, don't let her be forgotten and relegated to the back row of the balcony for my wedding or whatever other fancy events there are. I'm starting to realize the people of Ravenzario may see her as 'just the nanny,' but she's my world."

Tony smiled, knowing Nicklaus wouldn't see it. His first foray into giving orders was a good one, and it warmed Tony's heart to know he wanted to make sure the woman who'd given everything to protect him would be honored in a way she deserved. "I promise, Nicklaus. I'll make sure she's taken care of."

"Thank you."

They waited for another ten minutes by Tony's estimation before Michaela returned.

"There's a house not too far from here," she told them, pointing. "Maybe half a mile."

Tony walked to where Nicklaus sat on the other man. "Then let's go."

Michaela didn't think she'd ever been so wet in her life.

At least now they could use the flashlights on their phones to light the ground. It meant less chance of tripping. She still didn't know how none of them had been seriously injured during their first trip through the woods.

They found a trail that seemed to head the direction they were going, and they followed it until it opened into a clearing. Tony and Nicklaus stayed at the tree line with the prisoner while she went to the door. Tony was afraid all of them might freak the home owner out.

She rang the doorbell then wrapped her arms around herself as she shivered. Footsteps sounded through the interior of the house, and a woman's voice yelled at her to hold on. What else would she do?

The door finally opened and Michaela saw Mrs. Girabaldi, a

daily customer at the bakery, standing there. Relief flooded over her.

"Michelle! Dear, what happened? Get in here! We'll call the sheriff."

Michaela shook her head. "My son, Anthony, and I were attacked. They have the man at the edge of the woods but didn't want to scare whoever lived here. Do you have some rope I can use while you call the sheriff?"

Mrs. Girabaldi's eyes had grown wide as she listened. "Of course, dear. There's some in the shed. It's not locked. Go find it, then all three of you get yourselves in here."

"Thank you, ma'am." Michaela hurried back to where Anthony and Nicklaus could see her to wave them in. Within a few minutes, the man was hog-tied. Michaela, Nicklaus, and Anthony went inside while Mr. Girabaldi watched over the prisoner with his shotgun. Anthony stood where he could see both men on the porch with hot chocolate in his hand.

It took more time than she would have preferred for the sheriff to arrive, but it really wasn't long. They all went to the station. She didn't know what Anthony said to the authorities, but he seemed to believe the man would be extradited to Ravenzario without much trouble.

They made it back to the suite at Anthony's resort about the time daybreak hit.

Anthony closed the door behind him and looked at them both. "It's time," he said quietly. "There's a plane waiting for us at the airport. We can pack up your things here, and a team will be sent to Edwardsville to pack up everything you want to keep that you left behind."

She would sell the house. It was in her name - her fake name - but she wouldn't be able to live there. Just like she wouldn't want to live in Ravenzario with Nicklaus so close and so far away at the same time.

Nicklaus put an arm around her shoulders. "Are you ready for this, Mom?"

She squared her shoulders. "I've known it was coming for a long time. Our flight to Europe was to have taken off tomorrow."

Nicklaus didn't reply except to nod to Anthony.

Anthony seemed... something she couldn't quite put her finger on. Resigned? Stoic? The packing didn't take long, and soon they were seated in Anthony's car, driving toward the local airport. Anthony said the plane waiting for them wasn't the Ravenzarian royal plane, but rather the private jet belonging to the prince consort's family. To avoid questions they weren't ready to answer. She could tell Nicklaus was in awe of the luxuriousness of the plane, but he wouldn't admit it. She had raised him, though. She knew his expressions, his body language, and he wasn't quite sure what to make of all of it.

She sat next to him on a couch and buckled her seatbelt. "How're you feeling, Nicky?"

He just stared out the window. "I'm not sure. I'm glad you're okay, and that the guy has been arrested, but about the rest of it? Being a prince and all that? I don't know. What do I know about being a prince?"

"I couldn't teach you everything you needed to know about being a prince, but you've grown into a kind, considerate young man, and I think that goes a long way toward being a good prince, too."

She was assailed by sudden doubts. Again. Should she already be treating him like the prince he was? They were on their way back to Ravenzario, after all. Leaning her head against his shoulder, she decided she would relish these last few hours before they landed. Until then he could remain her "son" - her little boy all grown up.

A voice came over the loudspeaker. "Ladies and gentlemen, we'll be taking off in just a few moments. Please take your seats and buckle your seat belts." He went on to tell them they would be flying to Atlanta to refuel and then on to Ravenzario. "If you would like something to eat or drink, we have a fully stocked kitchen. Please feel free to help yourself. Otherwise, settle back and enjoy your flight."

The first part of the trip was quiet but not uncomfortable. After a little over an hour of staring out the window, Nicklaus turned to her.

"Tell me about Ravenzario."

"Do you remember studying it?" Michaela had made him study different countries around the world each summer. Every year, he studied a European country and at least one other. She picked the European countries, and he chose the others. She'd chosen Ravenzario twice and the entire Commonwealth of Belles Montagnes once. Had he put it together why she'd chosen those?

"I remember studying it, and you telling me you'd lived there, but not a ton of details. We looked at some current events and history through WWII, but never recent history. What's it like?"

Michaela leaned her head back against the seat. "I haven't lived there in a long time. From what I understand, Henry Eit, your mother's half-brother, may have changed some things quite a bit to line his own pockets."

"He's not Nicklaus's uncle."

Michaela and Nicklaus both turned to see Anthony standing beside them. She tried to assimilate what he'd said, but all she could come up with was, "What?"

Tony took a seat, hating the truth he had to tell both Nicklaus and Michaela. "Michaela, did King Richard ever tell you why he thought his children might be in danger?"

She shook her head. "No. He only told me he'd been made aware of a potential threat, and if I ever felt the need, to take the children and run. He seemed to think it would likely be some sort of catastrophic incident one of the children might survive. He was right, I guess. It was an accident, of course, but I always wondered if it might have been more than that."

"It was," Tony told her. "Henry was responsible for the accident, though we couldn't prove that until a few weeks ago. The greater impact was information that's also not been made public yet. Henry Eit may not be his legal name, but he also wasn't related to Queen Marissa after all. There'd been questions for a long time about parts of his history that didn't quite add up, but with his immense power as regent, we weren't able to confirm much until we found a treasure trove of paperwork after his re-arrest nearly two months ago. Once we did, we were able to confirm he's not actually related to the late queen. He was after revenge because of something your great-grandfather had done, Prince Nicklaus. His grandfather had his land confiscated because of some crimes he committed. Henry blamed your great-grandfather for the loss of his heritage and decided to take it out on your family. He'd planned to kill all four of you, but Queen Christiana's illness meant she wasn't in the car, but Michaela was instead. The car wouldn't have fit all five of you. Michaela would have been in one of the other vehicles in the motorcade."

He could see both of them try to absorb it all, but he continued. "I have long believed that Queen Christiana's illness wasn't just a way to save her life, but to save yours, too, Nicklaus, and probably yours, Michaela. The queen's bout with the flu is probably the best thing that could have happened to all three of you at that point."

Nicklaus looked dumbfounded. "How do you figure?"

"If Christiana was in the car, you would have been seated where Michaela was and far less likely to survive. Christiana would have been where you were and not in a car seat, so she would have been hurt worse. By being ill, she survived by not being in the crash, but both of you survived, too. Maybe not comfortably or easily at all times, but you survived."

Tony could tell they weren't entirely convinced, but hopefully, eventually, they'd see what he meant.

They didn't deplane in Atlanta and were there only long enough to refuel before taking off toward Ravenzario once more. Nicklaus and Michaela both tried to sleep. Tony slept some then caught up on paperwork and messaged with Duke Alexander. They would get in late enough that he would stay at a local hotel with Nicklaus and Michaela for the night. They'd see the queen first thing in the morning.

It wasn't until they were actually in that hotel suite that he had a chance to talk with Michaela alone again. Nicklaus was taking a shower. They all would head to bed shortly.

They'd snuck in a back door, and no one knew they were there except Duke Alexander and a couple of Tony's most trusted security team members who stood guard in the hallway. There were only a few rooms on this floor and the others were unoccupied. No one should see anything they shouldn't.

"Are you ready for all this?" Tony asked Michaela as she sipped on some tea.

"I always knew this day would come."

The prevarication wasn't lost on Tony. "That's not what I asked. Tomorrow, you'll no longer be the most important woman in his life."

Michaela took a deep breath as she waited for the doors to open. Nicklaus looked like he couldn't quite decide what he was supposed to be feeling. Excited? Nauseated? They seemed to be warring for primary position on his face. At least she was familiar with the palace. Nicklaus seemed to be in awe, though he tried not to show it. He didn't take them on a tour, but spent about twenty minutes in Tony's office he took care of a few things, including getting both of them the security passes they would need to access the palace.

Then it was time.

Tony looked at both of them. "Are you ready?"

Nicklaus blew out a deep breath. "As ready as I'll ever be."

Tony nodded to someone and the doors swung open, though she couldn't see who opened them.

Tears filled Michaela's eyes as she saw Queen Christiana for the first time in so long. The queen sat in a chair near the middle of the room. Duke Alexander stood at her side, his arms behind his back.

Tony bowed as he came to a stop in front of them. "Your

Majesty, Your Royal Highness, I have some people I would like you to meet."

The duke's eyes twinkled. He knew what was coming. The queen just looked puzzled. She nodded at Michaela, "You look familiar, ma'am, but I cannot quite place how. Tony, would you be so kind as to help me remember?"

"Of course. May I present Ms. Michaela Engel, lately of Edwardsville, Illinois in the United States, but a Ravenzarian by birth."

The queen's head tilted to the side. "I am afraid that is not quite enough information. Have we met?"

"Yes, ma'am." Michaela bobbed a curtsy. "I was your nanny many, many years ago."

She could see the confusion cross the queen's face again. "My nanny?" And the realization crossed her face. "You were in the car," she whispered, but her attention immediately shifted to Nicklaus. "Does that make you...?" The queen's voice broke, and she turned ghostly white.

Tony interceded. "Your Majesty, your brother, Prince Nicklaus of Ravenzario."

The queen sat slack-jawed for an eternity before she stood, tears streaming down her cheeks. "Nicky?" she whispered. "Is that really you?"

"So I'm told," he replied. "I confess I have no recollection of anything before we lived in Louisiana."

Christiana's hands covered her mouth as she walked toward him. She reached out and put both hands on either side of his face. "Nicky? Can it really be you?" she whispered.

"It is, Your Majesty. We had a DNA test done. It's him." Tony confirmed.

"Oh, Nicky!" She flung her arms around Nicklaus. "I can't believe it's really you!"

The queen held on to her brother, and he wrapped his arms around her.

The prince consort chuckled. "If she's using contractions then I'd say we succeeded in shocking her, Tony." He walked to Michaela and held out his hand. "Thank you, Ms. Engel, for doing everything you could to protect him since the accident."

She shook his hand. "It was my honor."

"I've known for a while that you two likely survived and put a private investigator friend on it. He couldn't find anything until Tony shared what little info he had. You did a very good job at hiding."

"King Richard set most of it up beforehand. I can't claim credit for much."

"Nonsense. You raised him into a fine young man. Since we found out the names you've been using, we've been doing some digging. You have done a fabulous job raising Nicklaus."

"That was the easy part of it." Michaela had always felt the escape was the hard part. Even then she'd only followed a preset plan.

"Don't sell yourself short, Michaela." Tony joined the conversation. "You're the one who traipsed through the frigid river with a toddler in your arms. You're the one who climbed up the other bank of that river and hid until you could get to the closest phone and call for help. You're the one who decided who to trust and who not to in those critical first days. You may not have done the planning or procured the false papers, but don't ever diminish what you did."

"He's right." She turned to see Nicklaus with his arm around Christiana's shoulder as she hugged his waist from the side. "I would have died that day or in one of the ones that followed, if it weren't for you. Remember the scare after I had my appendix out? Or when we found out I'm allergic to bees? Without you, either of those times, I would have died. You're the reason I'm still here today and not just because of what happened here in Ravenzario."

"You have my eternal gratitude, Mickey."

Michaela's vision blurred at the use of Christiana's old nickname for her. "It was my honor, Your Majesty. Truly."

With a small cry, Christiana let go of Nicklaus and flung herself at Michaela. "Thank you," the queen whispered as she held on tight. "I remember how much you loved us. When Tony told me your bodies had never been found, my heart broke at the thought of both of you in that water. I never even considered that a plan had been in place for your survival."

She let go and turned toward her husband. "You knew?"

Duke Alexander nodded. "I've known since your uncle was arrested the first time that there had been a plan in place. It wasn't until a few weeks ago that we knew for sure they had made it to Athmetis safely. Tony found them not long after."

The queen glared at her husband. "He was never my uncle." She looked at Tony. "Is this why you insisted on taking a vacation as soon as Henry went back to Pirate's Island?"

Tony nodded. "I had to. There wasn't much time."

"Wasn't much time?" Nicklaus asked the question.

Michaela knew the answer but had no desire to tell him.

"That's right." Christiana's words were barely more than a breath. "Your twenty-first birthday was last week."

Nicklaus nodded. "Yes. So?"

Queen Christiana glanced at her husband and back to her brother before answering. "The wedding is next Saturday."

Nicklaus looked puzzled. "What wedding?"

Christiana moved in front of him, holding out both hands. He clasped them, and she gave the answer Michaela had known was coming. The answer would rock Nicklaus even more than the news that he was a prince.

"*Your* wedding, Nicky. You're marrying Princess Yvette of Mevendia in eight days."

Tony could see the myriad of emotions play over Nicklaus's face.

Michaela moved to his side. "Remember Eve?"

He nodded. "You told me our fathers hoped we'd get married someday."

"It was more than that." Michaela guided him to a small sofa where they both sat down. "When you were young and Princess Yvette was born, they immediately decided they wanted the two of you to marry someday. It's been many generations since the families married one of their future monarchs to a member of the other family. The papers were drawn up. The contract is intact. It doesn't expire until a week after the wedding date, two weeks after the princess's birthday, and three weeks after yours."

Tony jumped in. "It was also part of the plan should Henry succeed in killing all of you. The contract, the details of which have never been fully made public, provided for Yvette to be queen if something were to happen to both of you."

"Even before the wedding?" Christiana asked, her arm resting on her belly.

"Yes. It was a safeguard against Henry. King Antonio would have acted as regent until she was of age. He tried to step in as regent anyway, but because of the way it was worded, it only applied if you were both killed. It never occurred to any of them that one of you might survive an attack that killed the other."

Nicklaus's jaw was clenched, but he managed to reply. "And it's somehow legally binding that I marry a girl that I've never met?"

Tony understood his skepticism. "I'm afraid so. Both legislatures validated the agreement, making it legally binding."

"And I can't appeal through the courts?" Nicklaus crossed his arms over his chest.

"This isn't the United States," Tony reminded him. "The court system here will not overturn the agreement or the legislative action approving it. You are legally a Ravenzarian subject, despite your claim to the throne and your life in the States."

Some kind of realization crossed Nicklaus's face as he turned to Michaela. "Is that why you never encouraged me to vote?"

Michaela nodded. "I didn't feel right about it, when neither of us were legally Americans. I couldn't even go to the embassies to try to get truly legal status. Too much risk."

Queen Christiana broke in. "Is he the legal monarch? We still have male primogeniture. He was to have been king. The only reason I was crowned queen was because of his death."

Tony sighed. "Why don't we all go somewhere we can be a bit more comfortable and maybe get some breakfast? I'll explain everything I know."

The queen put her arm around her brother's waist. His went around her shoulder as they all walked toward the apartments. Alexander had taken care of letting Paul, the head chef, know they would need something to eat, and a breakfast spread waited for them on the table in front of the windows overlooking the Mediterranean.

After they each had a full plate of food, Tony started to explain. "The leaders of Parliament were all on board with the marriage contract. It was celebrated by everyone in both countries. There were a few people who spoke out about the antiquated idea of a contract when you were so young, but overall the response was very positive. The general public believed the two of you would grow up knowing each other, and it would all work out just fine. Most people thought the contract would have been null and void upon your death, but a few people knew the truth. It's become fairly public in the last six months as Princess Yvette has planned the wedding with the help of Queen Christiana and Lizbeth Bence of Mevendia. Princess Yvette fully expects to be 'stood up at the altar,' though her father has always known there was a chance you survived."

"So the wedding is completely planned?" Michaela asked.

Alexander answered. "Yes. It's being held on my family's property not too far from here. I would imagine many of those invited are planning to attend for the train wreck factor, if nothing else. At least, the RSVPs seem to have rolled in at about the expected pace, despite the lack of groom. We couldn't wait to be sure you were alive, Prince Nicklaus."

"Why didn't you look for me sooner?" The prince took a bite of what Tony thought were the world's best cinnamon rolls. Even better than the ones at Millie's.

Tony answered that one. "Until we were sure we'd rounded up everyone who'd been working for Henry, we didn't feel we could take the risk."

Nicklaus turned to Michaela and asked the question Tony had known was coming. "We were supposed to come to Europe today. Why?"

Michaela sipped her coffee before answering. "You're right. We were going to London for a couple of days then here."

"For my wedding?"

Michaela whispered her answer. "Yes."

Tony could see Nicklaus struggle with that. "And that's why you always told me about Eve?"

She nodded, but Tony could see the tears on her cheeks. He reached toward her, under the table, and squeezed her hand where it rested on her leg.

"And what if I won't do it?" His understandably defiant attitude burdened Tony.

Tony sighed. "I'm afraid, if either you or Princess Yvette refuse, you'll both be exiled from the Commonwealth. I would imagine that wouldn't be too difficult for you, sir, but the princess won't be eighteen until tomorrow. She's never lived anywhere but the Mevendian palace." Tony closed his eyes and blew out a breath. "And I'm afraid it would apply to Michaela as well. All three of you would be exiled."

Nicklaus glared at him. "That's low, Tony."

He let go of Michaela's hand. "I know. Unfortunately, it's not my call. It's written into the legalities surrounding the marriage contract. It was ratified by both legislatures."

"Why would my father do that?" The question came from Queen Christiana.

Tony could only tell her what he'd pieced together over the years. King Antonio had never been open about the rationale either. "I believe it had to do with protecting all of you from Henry. I really can't say what the reasons might have been beyond that. I can only say with absolute certainty what the consequences are."

"And the legislature will not overturn those consequences?" The queen called for her assistant. "Diana, can you please summon Majority Leader Caruso and Minority Leader Michaels? It is a matter of some urgency."

Diana left, but Tony had to break it to them. "I've already spoken with them about the contract and the legislation. They were briefed on my mission before I left, and they were inclined to leave it as it is. I suppose something may have changed in the last few weeks, but I don't want you to get your hopes up."

Prince Alexander broke in. "I briefed them myself two days

ago. They're very reluctant to even bring it before the legislature. Though we're sure we've rounded up everyone we know of, we may never be certain we've completely eradicated the whole thing. Within those sections and codicils are protections for the royal family from other possible threats."

"So is Nicky the true monarch?" Queen Christiana asked.

Tony had to shake his head. "No. Despite male primogeniture, you are the rightful monarch."

Michaela struggled to keep the rest of the tears at bay. She'd never known the details of the contract, just that the king was very specific that if it was safe, she should bring Nicky back. If she still didn't believe it was safe on Nicky's twenty-first birthday, she was to take him to King Antonio of Mevendia. She hadn't told either Nicklaus or Tony that she had still been debating which one it would be.

But for King Richard to arrange it so that she and Yvette would both be exiled if Nicklaus refused to marry the princess? That sunk to a whole different level. She hadn't been back to Ravenzario in so many years, and she wanted to see her family, wanted to let them know she was alive. Spend time with them. Not be forced to head back to the States to never return.

"Basically, there was a law very quietly passed, using special procedures that didn't require approval by the regent, naming Christiana queen. The wording was very innocuous, mostly just 'Christiana is queen, and no one else can challenge her right to the throne.' News organizations or others who noticed, were told it was a just in case provision, in case someone decided to pull a Princess Anastasia Romanov kind of thing. That person, claiming to be Prince Nicklaus, would have no claim to the throne. Those in the know believed it possible Henry would find a child he could try to pass off as Nicklaus. It spelled out what would happen if something were to happen to you if you died without an heir. The throne would then pass to Princess Yvette."

Micheala looked at Nicklaus from under lowered lashes. He was trying to assimilate all of the information and figure out what it meant. They all were. Queen Christiana and her husband were exchanging a look Michaela couldn't interpret. Something about Princess Yvette becoming queen?

By unspoken agreement, they left the conversation of primogeniture and arranged marriages behind. The queen asked Nicklaus about his life, trying to learn everything she could about her brother in one meal. Once breakfast ended, Nicklaus and the queen went for a walk while Michaela, Tony, and Duke Alexander returned to the security offices. After looking over some paperwork for a few minutes, Alexander left. Michaela found herself alone with Tony.

He sat next to her. "How are you, Michaela? This has to be overwhelming."

She fiddled with the hem of her shirt. "It is. I'm not sure why I'm still here though. I've finished my job of protecting Prince Nicklaus and getting him safely here."

Tony reached for her hand. "You're still here because you're a part of all of this. You are, essentially, Nicklaus's mother. You belong here as much as any of us." He checked a text message on his phone. "I have something to show you." He stood and held open the door for her.

"What?" What could he possibly have to show her that she'd be interested enough in to stop this conversation?

"Just come with me."

Michaela had lived in the palace for several years, but she didn't know it as well as she wished she did. Tony led her to a part of it she'd never been familiar with. He opened the door to a small sitting room and stood to the side to let her in.

She gave him a puzzled glance before going around him. When

she saw who waited there, she gasped, her hands flying up to cover her mouth. "Mama! Daddy!" She flew across the room and into their waiting arms.

The three of them held onto each other, tears streaming down their cheeks. Her mother whispered, "I can't believe you're really alive" over and over again.

Eventually, they sat down on one of the couches with Michaela snuggled into her father's side.

"Can you tell us what happened?" her father asked. "Tony told us a little bit when we talked to him late last night, but not the whole story."

Michaela looked around, but Tony was nowhere to be seen. "You saw Tony last night?"

Her mother nodded. "We'd received a call from the palace letting us know that an official wanted to talk with us. We tried to get out of it, but they insisted. Tony arrived fairly late last night and sat us down in the living room. He told us he had some news that would shock us then said you were alive. He didn't want us to see you for the first time and pass out from the shock."

"Neither of us slept a wink," her father admitted. "We wanted to drive straight to the hotel but we also understood the need to explain everything to the queen first."

"She and Nicky are off catching up somewhere."

Michaela could feel her father's chuckle. "Does that make us royal grandparents somehow?"

"I doubt it." She wanted to voice her fears to them, but she couldn't bring herself to.

"We want to hear everything," her mother said. "We've never been to the States."

"I'll tell you all about it, but it'll take a lot more time than we have now." Another thought hit her. "Where are Marla and Joe?"

"Marla and her family are in Athmetis on vacation. Tony said he was arranging for them to be brought back later today. Joseph and his family moved to southern Ravenzario a few months ago. I'm sure they'll come as soon as they hear."

"I've stalked their Facebook pages some," Michaela admitted. "I've seen the public pictures of you guys, of her family, but there's not many. I didn't know about Dustin and his family until yesterday. I didn't look that closely." Tears threatened one more time.

"It was hard," her father admitted.

"When do we get to take you home?" her mother asked, tears trickling down her cheeks again.

"Not for a while I'm afraid." Tony walked into the room. "The wedding is in a week. Once this news becomes public, I would imagine there will be a lot of press camped out on your doorstep. In fact, it might be best for all of you, including your brother and sister's families, to stay here for the time being. There may be a few crazies out there." He frowned, an expression Michaela was coming to know well. Concern over the safety of those he felt responsible for. "If you'd prefer to stay at your own home, I'll arrange for security there as well."

Her mother and father glanced at each other. "It would probably be best for Michaela to stay here," her father told Tony. "We would prefer to stay with her, if it's not too much trouble."

Tony chuckled as he glanced at Michaela with a look she couldn't quite read. Excitement? She would get to see him a fair bit more if she stayed here at the palace than if she went to her parents' home. And if she went home with her parents, word of her crash survival would leak out before they were ready.

"I'm quite certain the queen would insist on it, Poppo. You aren't to leave without seeing her."

Poppo? Wasn't that how he'd been listed in the wedding program?

"Did she know?" Her father's voice contained the shock Michaela felt.

"No, sir. She has no idea you're related to Mickey. I don't know that she ever knew."

Her father's eyes filled with tears of his own. "When I first saw her last year, it was so hard not to ask her, but I would do nothing to bring her more pain. She doesn't remember meeting me a time or two as a very young child. I couldn't tell her I was Michaela's father, or about my son and the bridge."

"I won't tell her until you're ready, sir."

"Thank you."

"If you want to get whatever you need, we'll get all three of you set up in a suite. Your siblings and their families will be welcome, too."

With that decided, her parents reluctantly left to pack a few things. Michaela and Tony were left alone in the room.

Tony looked at her and she could see the weight of the world on his shoulders. "We need to talk."

Tony had seen enough of the initial meeting to know it was everything Michaela would have hoped for. He'd seen her parents faces the night before when he'd told them she was alive. Telling them ahead of time had been the right move. Someone keeling over from a heart attack because of the shock would be a bad idea.

"What is it?" Michaela seemed defeated. He could empathize. So much had changed for her in the last forty-eight hours, in the last few weeks.

He smiled and moved to stand in front of her, his hands landing on her hips. "It's nothing quite so dire." She slid her arms around his waist and rested her head on his chest. "We're planning to go to Mevendia first thing in the morning. We need to let them know that Nicklaus is alive. He asked if you were going. I told him it was up to you."

Michaela moved away from him to stare out one of the windows. "No. It's time for Nicklaus to do things without me."

"You'll always be his family," Tony reminded her. Did she really think the last eighteen years of raising him would disappear out the window?

"Maybe, but it's time for him to become part of the Ravenzarian royal family. I am not, and never will be, a family member. I've known that since I took the job twenty years ago."

Tony wanted to protest, but he knew only Nicklaus could convince her. He believed the young prince would, but it would take time and reassurance for Michaela to truly understand how much she meant to Nicklaus.

"Let's talk about something else." He took her hand and turned her around. "Like how glad I am you're here with me."

She gave him a shy smile before staring at his chest. "But what if Nicklaus doesn't go through with the wedding? I won't be able to stay. Until we know what's going to happen, I think we should table any discussions about us."

"If he decides not to stay, and you return to the States, I'm not sure I could stay either."

Michaela still didn't look at him. "You barely know me."

"I know enough to know I want to get to know you better. I also know enough to know I think the restrictions are ridiculous."

"You won't quit your job for me."

"I would, but I may not have to. If Prince Nicklaus decides he won't marry Princess Yvette, he'll still need protecting. I would count it an honor to be in charge of that. Even if I'm not asked or allowed to, I don't know that I would stay here."

She didn't answer, and Tony decided not to push her before she was ready. What would the prince decide? He checked his phone. Time to find out.

"Prince Nicklaus has asked to meet with all of us in about fifteen minutes. He's asked for your parents to be there. They were stopped before they left the palace grounds."

She simply nodded but still said nothing. After a moment, she turned and finally spoke. "Let's go."

The most important decision of her life, and Michaela couldn't even make it herself.

Instead, she sat at a conference table in the queen's office, with her parents on one side and empty seats on the other. Queen Christiana sat at the head of the table with her husband on one side and her brother on the other.

"We have a few things to discuss," she began. "First Poppo and Nanny, you have my deepest gratitude. I cannot imagine how difficult the last years have been for you. I also know you raised a daughter who put everything aside to protect me and my brother. She gave everything to protect him, and without the values you instilled in her, he might not be here and alive."

Her parents murmured their thanks, though Michaela knew they didn't believe it was necessary.

"I do not know how I never put the last names together. It never occurred to me you had the same last name as my nanny."

Her father took the queen's hand. "We didn't want to cause you any more pain, sweet girl." He looked at her the same way he'd looked at Michaela. It warmed her heart to know that, for the last year at least, her father had been looking after her young charge.

The queen smiled at him and squeezed his hand before turning to Michaela. "Second, Mickey, I have not decided how to publicly thank you for all you have done, but, rest assured, when the time comes I will do so."

Michaela felt her face flush. "I didn't do it for the thanks, ma'am." She'd changed the queen's nappies. How odd to be calling her ma'am. "It was the right thing to do."

"Nevertheless, when the time comes, the country will know how indebted to you we are." She turned to her brother. "Soon, we will need to hold a press conference detailing your survival, but first, we need to visit Mevendia. The Van Renssalaer family needs to be told immediately that you are, indeed, still alive. I have been recently informed..." She sent her husband and Tony, on his other side, a disapproving glare. "...that King Antonio knew there was a plan in place and that Henry likely was not trustworthy. I am also aware the Mevendian and Montevarian governments have lent any assistance they could whenever it was required. Antonio and his family, especially Yvette, need to know that things have changed and what your plans are." She gave Nicklaus a far more tender look. "Have you decided yet, Nicky?"

He took a deep breath and blew it out slowly. "I would like to meet Yvette first, talk to her. Right now, I just don't know."

Relief washed over Michaela. At least he wasn't refusing. Maybe she wouldn't have to leave her beloved country nearly as soon as she arrived. A glance at Tony showed him looking at her, hope shining from his eyes.

The queen drew the attention back to herself. "I am relieved you are not ruling it out completely. I could not bear it if you were exiled and be unable to do anything about it."

Tony took over. "In the morning, the queen, Prince Nicklaus, and Prince Alexander will fly to Mevendia. I will accompany them and go over security measures for the wedding with their team."

Nicklaus turned to look at her. "Will you come, Michaela?"

She shook her head. "No, Nicky. It's not appropriate for me to go. I'll be waiting here when you get back."

The meeting continued for a few more minutes. Michaela hugged her parents one more time before they left to pack for a few days at the palace. The queen took Nicklaus's arm, and they left together. Likely to do more catching up. Alexander and Tony talked quietly for a few minutes. Michaela didn't know what she was supposed to do.

Finally, Tony walked around the table to her, holding out a hand. She took it and he helped her stand.

"Will you go for a walk with me?"

"You don't have anything else you're supposed to be doing?"

He grinned. "Nope. Not at the moment. I don't have a lot of time before I do need to get some things done to be ready for tomorrow morning, though." He squeezed her hand. "I want to spend some time with you before things get too crazy." He held open a door for her. She knew this one led to one of the small gardens. "I doubt we'll be in Mevendia very long. I'd guess we'll be home by dinner at the latest, and lunch is probably more realistic. But the wedding is in eight days. Until it's over, I doubt I'll have much free time. I've kept an eye on things, but the queen has been my primary concern until now."

"As it should have been."

He linked his fingers with hers as they rounded a large bush of some kind. There was a bench there, hidden from the prying eyes found around a palace. They sat down and Tony turned to her. He brushed her hair back from her face.

"It's probably too soon to tell you this, Michaela, but I don't care. Once things settle down after the wedding, I want to court you. Not long after that, I want to ask you to marry me."

Michaela's breath caught in her chest at the words and the earnest look on his face. "You do?" she whispered.

"I do." He winked. "I even went so far to ask your son what he thought about it."

He asked Nicklaus? "What did he say?"

"He wanted to know what took me so long."

"We've known each other a month." And Tony already knew?

"And he's probably going to marry a girl he'll know a week. Sometimes, you know it's right even if everyone else would tell you you're crazy."

The thoughts tumbled around in her mind until the words came out. "Yes. I want that, too."

Tony leaned toward her. "Good." His breath teased her hair. "Then I'm going to kiss you before real life comes back to interfere again."

Michaela didn't have time to respond before his lips met hers. A feeling of rightness settled over her like a blanket on a cool evening.

She'd asked God, many times, if she'd ever find someone to love her. It couldn't have happened until Nicklaus no longer needed her protection, but she couldn't have imagined it happening so quickly once her son had returned to his rightful place as prince of Ravenzario.

Thoughts of Nicklaus fled as Tony pulled her closer. In the arms of a man charged with protecting the crown, in working together to protect the prince, she found someone worthy of protecting her heart.

Prince from her Past

Pounding on the door to her bedroom woke Princess Yvette Alexandra Charlotte Abigail of Mevendia from a dead sleep.

"What?" she yelled, praying it wasn't either of her parents. She'd be read the riot act for replying that way, though she had no way of knowing it was them and - she checked - she didn't have to be up for another hour.

"Your highness? Your father needs you to meet him in the throne room in an hour." Melinda, her personal assistant, walked over to the windows and pressed the button to open all of the curtains. Pinkish light from the dawn filled the room. And it was her birthday. No one should have to be up so early on her birthday. "He gave specific instructions."

"What's this about?" Yvette covered her head with her pillow.

"I don't know, miss. I believe the queen of Ravenzario is here on business, and he wants the whole family there."

Right. Yvette wanted to harbor feelings of snark toward her distant cousin, but found herself unable to. Orphaned by the car accident that took the life of Yvette's fiancé, Christiana had grown up with their mutual distant family members in Montevaro. At eighteen, she'd gained full control of the throne, hers only because of the death of her brother. The old rules of primogeniture still applied in Ravenzario, which meant Yvette would have been queen had Nicklaus lived. But Christiana had survived and should have been her sister-in-law in a week.

A national holiday had been declared in two countries.

The dress designed. The flowers ordered. Cake tasted. Invitations sent.

Nearly eighteen years earlier, her father had signed her life away. A marriage contract with the Crown Prince of Ravenzario. The wedding date had been set long before her first birthday and the contract had been written in such a way that it wasn't officially "broken" until two weeks after her birthday, a week after the wedding.

She'd asked about it a few times in the last few years. Why was she still engaged to a prince who died in a car accident in the last century? Her father had been terribly closed mouthed about it. And in five days, they'd head to Ravenzario where she'd get ready for the wedding, wait in an ante room, and when the groom failed to appear, head home in humiliation.

Yvette sat cross-legged on her bed, covers still pulled onto her lap.

If only she didn't love the dress so much. And the flowers. And everything else. She'd been able to choose whatever she wanted without a groom to interfere. Only her mother, the queen. And the protocol office. And a bunch of other stuffed shirts who wouldn't let her play a dirge as a wedding march, even though everyone knew this wedding wasn't actually going to happen.

And Lizbeth Bence. Really, Lizbeth had planned much of Yvette's wedding for her.

"Is the prince consort with her?" Yvette yawned as she swung her feet over the side of the bed.

"I don't know."

She'd met Duke Alexander several times and liked him. He'd even been her escort a time or two for official events in Ravenzario. However, Yvette hadn't seen him since the revelation of his teenage foray into acting became public. She'd binge watched *2 Cool 4 School*, a teen comedy starring Alexander and his twin brother, Christopher, after the news came out.

"Here we go." Melinda walked back into the bedroom carrying one of the dresses Yvette loathed. Midnight blue, cinched waist, short train. Heels were a must. Yvette hated heels. Whoever invented them should have been banished to Antarctica for life. "You need to take a quick shower, miss. Wash your hair, and Belinda will be in shortly to do it for you."

Belinda and Melinda. Twin sisters Yvette didn't know what she'd do without. "Thanks, Melinda." It wasn't her fault the king was obnoxious this early in the morning. A quick shower, a longer hair session, and quick bite to eat later - an hour after the pounding on the door - Yvette was ready to go. As much as she hated dressing up in general, she had to admit, she felt nice wearing it.

Her heels clicked along the stone floor as she made her way to the throne room. Her father rarely conducted business in there, so why was he doing it now? Something to do with the wedding? Maybe they'd call the whole farce of a thing off.

"You're here." Before she fully entered the throne room, her father's voice boomed her direction. "The rest of the family is on their way."

Because of where they were and the staff watching, Yvette dropped a slight curtsy toward her father before kissing his cheek. "Everyone is coming?" If both of her older brothers, her sister-in-law, and her mother would be there, this was big. Whatever it was.

"Yes. Christiana called in the middle of the night and asked for an immediate audience with the entire family. Her plane arrived a few moments ago."

The door behind her opened again and the rest of the family

entered. Her brothers looked especially handsome in their uniforms, complete with swords and sashes. Jessabelle, her sister-in-law, looked more uncomfortable than Yvette had seen her in a long time. That wedding had been planned in less than two weeks, and Jessabelle had met Malachi at the altar. Yvette still didn't quite understand the forces behind the suddenness of that arranged marriage, though it was indirectly responsible for a turnaround in her father.

The protocol minister bustled in behind her mother. "They have arrived. Please take your places."

Her father was already seated on the throne. Her mother sat next to him. The children all had assigned spots. Yvette moved to hers as Malachi whispered to his wife, kissing her temple in a move that made Yvette long to be loved like her brother obviously loved his wife, no matter their beginning.

The exceptionally large double doors at the other end of the room were opened by white-gloved doormen. A voice boomed from somewhere unseen.

"Christiana, Queen of Ravenzario, and Alexander, Duke of Testudines, and guest."

Christiana, with her gorgeous blond curls falling around her shoulders, led the way with Alexander just behind. Yvette couldn't see the guest.

Christiana stopped a few feet in front of the throne. "Thank you for agreeing to see us on such short notice, King Antonio."

He waved her off. "My pleasure. But it is early, and I don't believe my family has eaten, so can we get down to business? We would be honored if you would join us for a meal afterward."

"It would be our pleasure." Christiana stepped forward just a bit, and Alexander seemed to fade into the background, giving Yvette the first glimpse of the guest.

Wavy brown hair, lips that threatened to twitch into an easy grin at any moment, and twinkling eyes captivated her. He was easily the most handsome man she'd ever seen.

Bar none.

Including her very handsome brothers and Alexander in his teen heartthrob days.

"King Antonio, Queen Alicia, Prince William, Prince Malachi, Princess Jessabelle, and..." Christiana turned to look straight at her. "Princess Yvette. There is someone I would like you to meet."

She stepped to the side, and the guest moved forward.

"My brother. Prince Nicklaus of Ravenzario."

Nick stared at the young woman he was supposed to marry. All the color had drained from her face, and she looked like she might faint.

Definitely not his goal for this first meeting.

The woman standing on the other side of the room moved unobtrusively behind the throne until she was at the younger woman's side. She slid an arm around Yvette's waist. At least he presumed the pretty, suddenly-pale, girl was Yvette. She matched the pictures Michaela kept around the house, though the most recent one had been several years old. The deep blue of her dress didn't help her skin tone any. In fact, the word "alabaster" came to mind.

The king drew Nick's attention back to the chair dominating the end of the long room. "Excuse me?"

Nick's new-found sister stared down the king. "You heard me, Antonio."

The king didn't look too pleased at the use of his name without the title in front of it. But Christiana was a queen in her own right. She may have been the younger generation, but she didn't let the king intimidate her.

Nick kept his eyes on the slip of a girl who seemed to be struggling to stand. Had she not been told there was even a possibility he was still alive? He didn't quite understand all of the dynamics that led to his escape with Michelle...Michaela. Would he ever get her real name straight in his head?

King Antonio ran his hand down his face. "Why don't we go have breakfast? This isn't the official conversation I thought it would be."

"What did you think it would be?" Christiana rested her hands on her expanding stomach. "That I was going to tell you no trace had been found?"

She was bluffing. Nick knew his sister had no idea where Tony had been. She truly believed her head of security had been on vacation, not tracking down the long-missing heir to the throne and his nanny.

"To be honest? Yes. I think all of us who knew of the escape plan believed contact would have been made long ago if the plan had been successful."

"You knew?" The whisper came from the girl to the side. "You knew he might be alive and you never told me? You didn't think I had a right to know?"

Antonio stood and walked toward her, enveloping her in a hug when he reached her. "Why don't we go change into something more comfortable. We'll have breakfast? And we'll talk it through then."

Princess Yvette nodded. "Okay," she whispered, the sound echoing through the large room. She turned and froze as his eyes met hers.

Nick smiled his best smile. He didn't want to scare her any more than she probably already was. He was also sure she didn't know what would happen if the wedding didn't take place. The only reason he still even considered going through with a wedding to someone he'd never met. That the three of them would be exiled if they didn't.

The Mevendian royal family all left with Nick, his sister, and brother-in-law trailing behind.

They were ushered into a formal dining room unlike any Nick had ever seen. He amended the thought. Not since he was a very young child. He'd been born Crown Prince Nicklaus, but he'd been raised solidly middle class American. This kind of dining room didn't exist in his world until a few days earlier.

It took nearly half an hour, filled mostly with uncomfortable silence between him and the family he didn't really know, for the Mevendian family to come back in. By then, food was being brought in as well.

"I suppose introductions are in order." King Antonio started as a plate was delivered. He pointed to the queen, seated to his right. Then his oldest son, William, and so on around the table until he got to the teenage girl, now dressed in nice slacks and a filmy top of some kind. "And, of course, my daughter, Princess Yvette. Your fiancée."

Nick smiled and nodded at her. "A pleasure to meet you."

She looked like she was going to cry and didn't say anything.

Before anyone else could, the door opened behind Nicklaus.

"I heard there was a family breakfast going on."

He turned to see an older woman, not very tall, walking in like she owned the place. Come to think of it, she likely had at one point, if she was a member of this royal family.

She came to a stop next to him, and before he realized what she was doing, her cool hands were on either side of his face. "Welcome home, Prince Nicklaus. We've been waiting for you."

He blinked as a servant pulled out the chair next to him, and she took a seat. "You've been waiting for me? You knew I was alive? *I* didn't even know I was alive." Well, that came out wrong.

But she just chuckled. "Oh, yes. I knew." She waved a hand toward the king. "Not in any official capacity, but I did know, in my heart of hearts, that Prince Nicklaus would be found."

"Why didn't you tell me, Nana Yvette?"

Nick could see the tender look on Nana Yvette's face. "It

wasn't time yet, my dear one. Just like it wasn't time for anyone to know about Malachi or Jessabelle until last year."

Who? Right. The king's second son and his wife, both now staring at their plates. That was a thread to be pulled at later.

Then Nana Yvette turned to him. "Why don't you tell us your story, Nicklaus? How did you manage to survive the accident, and where have you been all these years?"

Nick put down his fork and used his napkin to wipe his mouth. "I don't remember much of it," he admitted. "Just what my mother and Tony told me this week."

"Your mother?" The question came from the king.

Right. He needed to be more careful. A glance at his sister showed her studying her plate very carefully, her lips in a tight line.

"Michelle, that is. Michaela." Would he ever get it right? He reached over and squeezed his sister's hand. "Michaela, our nanny, went by Michelle. She never made it a secret that I wasn't her child, but I believed she was my aunt, raising me after the death of my parents. I hated not having a mother, and it kept up our pretense for me to call her mom most of the time. We rarely corrected those who didn't know any better. Those who knew us well enough knew what I believed to be the truth about the relationship."

He squeezed Christiana's hand again before letting it go. "I didn't know my sister was still living until a few weeks ago. I don't remember the escape or the journey to the United States. I just found out about the wedding this week. I always knew there was this girl, Eve, that my parents had hoped I'd marry, but I didn't know about the contract or the exiles until very recently."

"Exiles?" Princess Yvette looked at him then her father. "Who's being exiled?"

King Antonio set down his fork. "If this wedding does not happen, both of you and Michaela will be exiled from the Commonwealth."

Available Now!

Princess Yvette of Mevendia has been engaged since before her first birthday. Thanks to the ridiculous contract her father signed, the engagement is still intact and the wedding set to occur a week after her eighteenth birthday, even though the groom's been dead for over seventeen years.

Or has he?

Prince Nicklaus of Ravenzario and his nanny narrowly escaped death when a car accident claimed the lives of his parents. Raised in hiding in the United States, and recently informed of his royal heritage, Nicklaus has returned to the land of his birth just in time for his wedding.

Nicklaus finds himself attracted to Princess Yvette, but is that enough to go through with the wedding? Or will he suffer banishment not only for himself, but the nanny who raised him and the fiance he's only just met? Despite his tall, dark, and handsome appeal, Yvette isn't sure she wants to go through with the wedding - but she really doesn't want to be exiled either. She prefers to be proactive, to go after what she wants, but this time, the princess finds her future, her chance at happiness, in the hands of the prince from her past.

ABOUT THE AUTHOR

When she's not writing about her imaginary friends, USA Today Bestselling Author Carol Moncado prefers binge watching pretty much anything to working out. She believes peanut butter M&Ms are the perfect food and Dr. Pepper should come in an IV. When not hanging out with her hubby, four kids, and two dogs who weigh less than most hard cover books, she's probably reading in her Southwest Missouri home.

Summers find her at the local aquatic center with her four fish, er, kids. Fall finds her doing the band mom thing. Winters find her snuggled into a blanket in front of a fire with the dogs. Spring finds her sneezing and recovering from the rest of the year.

She used to teach American Government at a community college, but her indie career, with over twenty titles released, has allowed her to write full time. She's a founding member and former President of MozArks ACFW, blogger at InspyRomance, and is represented by Tamela Hancock Murray of the Steve Laube Agency.

www.carolmoncado.com
books@candidpublications.com

The CANDID Romance Series

Finding Mr. Write
Finally Mr. Write
Falling for Mr. Write

The Monarchies of Belles Montagnes Series
(Previously titled The Montevaro Monarchy
and The Brides of Belles Montagnes series)

Good Enough for a Princess
Along Came a Prince
More than a Princess
Hand-Me-Down Princess
Winning the Queen's Heart
Protecting the Prince (Novella)
Prince from her Past

Serenity Landing Second Chances

Discovering Home
Glimpsing Hope
Reclaiming Hearts

Crowns & Courtships

Heart of a Prince
The Inadvertent Princess
A Royally Beautiful Mess

Crowns & Courtships Novellas

Dare You

A Kaerasti for Clari

Serenity Landing Tuesdays of Grace
9/11 Tribute Series

Grace to Save

Serenity Landing Lifeguards
Summer Novellas

The Lifeguard, the New Guy, & Frozen Custard
(previously titled: The Lifeguards, the Swim Team, & Frozen Custard)
The Lifeguard, the Abandoned Heiress, & Frozen Custard

Serenity Landing Teachers
Christmas Novellas

Gifts of Love
Manuscripts & Mistletoe
Premieres & Paparazzi

Mallard Lake Township

Ballots, Bargains, & the Bakery (novella)

Timeline/Order for Crowns & Courtships and Novellas
1. *A Kaerasti for Clari*
2. *Dare You*
(the first two can be read in either order, but technically this is the timeline)
3. *Heart of a Prince*
4. *The Inadvertent Princess*
5. *A Royally Beautiful Mess*

22635770R00083

Made in the USA
Columbia, SC
03 August 2018